HUGE pain in my ████!

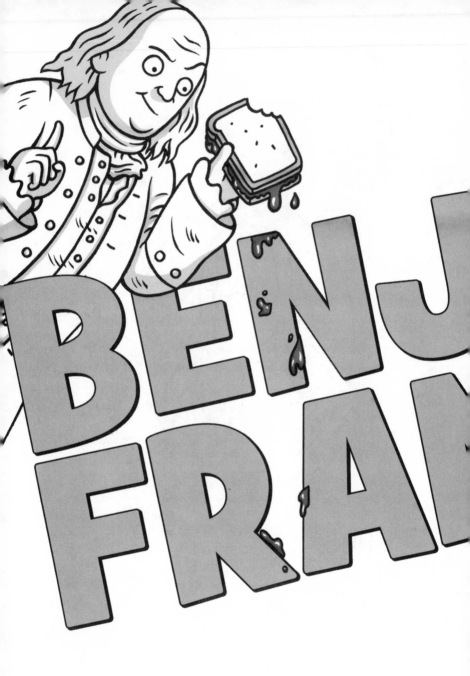

Printed in the United States of America
First Edition, September 2015
1 3 5 7 9 10 8 6 4 2

FAC-020093-15166

Designed by Tyler Nevins

Library of Congress Cataloging-in-Publication Data

Mansbach, Adam, 1976-
    Benjamin Franklin huge pain in my *** / Adam Mansbach & Alan Zweibel.—First
edition.
        pages ; cm
    Summary: In the midst of adjusting to middle school and having a girlfriend, Franklin
"Ike" Saturday's life becomes even more complicated when he writes a letter to Benjamin
Franklin as an extra-credit assignment and gets a reply, beginning a correspondence that
could change history.
    ISBN 978-1-4847-1304-4
[1. Middle schools—Fiction. 2. Schools—Fiction. 3. Dating (Social customs)—Fiction.
4. Franklin, Benjamin, 1706-1790—Fiction. 5. Letters—Fiction. 6. Stepfamilies—
Fiction. 7. United States—History—Revolution, 1775-1783—Fiction. 8. Humorous
stories.] I. Zweibel, Alan. II. Title.
    PZ7.1.M367Ben 2015
    [Fic]—dc23        2015004694

Reinforced binding
Visit www.DisneyBooks.com

For my beautiful grandchildren:
Zachary, Lexi, Jordan, and Kylie
—A.Z.


For The Jazz Wolf
—A.M.

# CHAPTER 1

April 5, 2015

Dear Mr. Franklin,

First of all, let me just say that this Assignment is Stupid. You are Dead. Why am I writing a letter to Some dead guy I've never even met? For an answer, you'd have to ask Mr. Larrapin, who is my seventh-grade History Teacher and what us Teenagers of the twenty-first century would call a Grade A doofusburger. He's not even going to Read the letters. I could seal a two-for-one coupon for Little Caesars Pizza in this envelope, and as long as I spelled your name right and sealed it with Old-Timey Candle Wax, he would give me the Extra Credit.

I am Capitalizing Random Words to Make You Feel At Home in this letter because I have Noticed that that is what you did in your Day. I am not going to make the s's look like f's like you guys did, because That is just too Annoying. So tough Luck.

Before you get too Flattered that I am writing You, out of all the Historical Figures in History, let me point out that I am mainly Writing to say: Thanks a lot. Which is Sarcasm, because what I really mean is not Thanks for inventing electronic kites or the Post Office, but thanks for being such a Big-Shot Inventor and Diplomat and Guy Who Walked Around Philly Eating a Loaf of Bread for Some Reason that my dad decided, "Hey, Ben Franklin is awesome. I'm gonna Name my kid after him."

Maybe that doesn't sound so bad to You. Maybe you're thinking, Benjamin is a Smashing Name for a Lad, or whatever. But my name isn't Ben, you stringy-haired old Windbag. My name is Franklin. Which might be a decent name for a medium-sized dog, but let me tell you: it is a Terrible Name for a Person.

Franklin Isaac Saturday. That's my name, if you can believe It. Maybe that would have flown in Colonial Times, but these days it is more than enough to Get you Beat Up, even if you are not also Small for your Age and Not Great at sports, which are some of my other Characteristics, though—don't get me wrong—I'm not a klutz or anything. I don't get picked Last in gym class like some Loser Kid in a Book. I get picked toward the End of the Middle, and I have Kissed two girls. Which sounds like a Typical Night for you, huh, Mr. Franklin? Word on the interwebs is that you were quite the Ladies' Man in your Day. If you are surprised that a kid of the Future knows this type of dirt about you, well, I'm sorry to Break the News. You are lucky you're Dead because these days a whole bunch of Cable News Shows would be camped out in front of your house, and you wouldn't be able to Waddle around, stuffing your Face with Bread.

The only time anybody hears the Franklin part of my name is on the First Day of school, when the teachers Take attendance and use whatever name is on the List, and I try to say "I go by Ike" as fast as Possible. This year Especially, because instead of a grade school, where everybody knows each other Anyway, I am in Junior High, and Five-Sixths of the kids went to other grade schools, and we have now been Dumped All Together like ingredients in a Big Stew and Mixed Up. And somehow, while us dudes were still trying to find our lockers, all the Girls got together and Figured Out, in like Seven Nanoseconds, which guys were going to be Popular in the New World of Thomas J. Harden Junior High. Basically what happened is that these three girls named Allie, Jennifer, and Melissa, who all came from different elementary schools but went to summer camp together or something, decided to have a party the second week of school at Allie's house and only invite the guys they thought were "hot." And so all the guys who were invited were like, "Duh, I guess these other 'hot' dudes are my new buddies." And just like that, everything got all scrambled up, and certain guys who'd been friends since nursery school, like me and Ryan Demphill, were suddenly divided from each other because they were part of different groups—groups they didn't even have any say in making up.

Do you believe that, Ben Franklin? I mean, would you stop hanging out with, say, John Hancock because some clique of girls you barely knew didn't think he was cool? Would you tell him that you just don't have as much in

# HUGE pain in my ▒▒▒

common anymore, because his idea of a Friday night is sitting at home watching Simpsons reruns with his little sister, and yours is playing spin the bottle in Alana Shoenfeld's basement and French-kissing random eighth-grade girls?

I bet you wouldn't. You guys never would have gotten the Constitution written if you'd let girls turn you into a bunch of idiots. You'd bring him along, wouldn't you? You'd tell the girls, "John Hancock is my friend, and he's cooler than any of you. Now, spin that freaking bottle like your life depends on it." And then it would stop right in front of Claire Wanzandae, and John Hancock would smooch the heck out of her. And you'd be like, "Dang, Hancock, maybe YOU oughta be Ambassador to France, if you know what I mean."

All right, Ben Franklin, that's about all I've got to say. Enjoy being dead. At least you're not in junior high.

Sincerely, your angry namesake,
Franklin


P.S.—You'll be glad to know that people still use a bunch of those little sayings you made up, like "A stitch in time saves nine." Although nobody has any idea what they mean. That one, especially. I'm guessing you were drunk when you said that.

P.P.S.—That's another thing, by the way: I have never been drunk. Me and Ryan chugged two wine coolers he stole from his sister Joanna last summer, but they just made me feel like I never wanted to taste artificial coconut flavoring ever again. According to Ryan, though, everybody gets drunk on Jungle Juice now and it's rad. Jungle Juice is when you take little bits of liquor from all your parents' bottles, so they don't notice that any is gone, and mix them together. I said that sounded disgusting, and he grinned this kind of sideways grin and said, "Yeah, dude, but it makes the chicks lose control." I told him he sounded like a slimeball, and he told me I didn't know thing the first about girls, and I shut up because that's true. But what do you think, BF? That's pretty sleazy even by your standards, right?

# CHAPTER 2

I don't usually dork out on school-related stuff, but it was 6:37 P.M. Saturday when I finished writing the letter, and my only other option was to ask my mom or Dirk the Jerk, my evil stepfather, for a ride to the Loews movie theater in Wynnewood so I could mill around in the lobby with Ryan and about sixteen hundred thousand other kids from my school and the other junior high in town.

You don't actually see a movie. You just sort of hang out, maybe eating Twizzlers and staring at some group of girls you want to talk to but not talking to them. And they're staring at you, too. Or at Ryan and his new bros, anyway. And they're laughing too loud and standing in these posey kinds of ways to attract as much attention as possible, and you're doing the same thing, only instead of the posiness

it's horsing around and punching each other in the arm
and stuff like that. And everybody wants the same thing, to
talk to each other, but instead you've got to go through this
whole elaborate ritual, like you're some weird species of bird
from the Discovery Channel or whatever. Maybe there's
some point to it that guys like the guy Ryan is turning into
understand. I know I don't.

And meanwhile, the ushers and the box office guys are
staring daggers at all of you because, duh, this is a movie
theater—buy a ticket or get out. And eventually they do
make you leave, but there's nowhere to go and nobody's
parents are coming until ten, when the movie you're supposedly seeing ends. So you just mill around outside, where they
have these stone benches—actually, everybody is waiting for
that because outside there's less space, so your group might
get mushed up against a group of girls, and then you can
start talking to them kind of accidentally. Or maybe there
will be a fight.

So that was if I wanted to go out. Meanwhile, my little
sister, Carolyn, was trying to get me to play Chutes and
Ladders with her, which is a rad way to spend Saturday night
if you're five, but pretty lame otherwise, which was why Dirk
the Jerk and Mom had already told her, "Maybe later, sweetie."

HUGE pain in my ░░░░░!

I figured I might as well make my letter look as good as possible, seeing as (a) I'd already taken the time to write it, and (b) I had nothing better to do. So I went into the yard and hunted around the bird feeder for a decent-sized feather to use as a quill, thinking I could do the address old-timey-style by breaking open a cheap pen and dipping the feather in ink. Dirk the Jerk has about a million pens because he's a sales rep for a bunch of drug companies, and they make these really ugly ballpoints with the drugs' names on them to give out to doctors—as if any doctor has ever been like, "Hmm, let's see. Should I prescribe Xeyltronex to this guy? On one hand, the side effects include mild dizziness, violent diarrhea, eyeballs growing on your gums, and instantaneous death, but on the other hand, I did get this cool five-cent pen from the drug rep, who also happens to look exactly like a fat, bald version of Robert Downey Jr., so why not?"

Carolyn came into the yard with me. She kept saying "Here, Ikey," and handing me these tiny little downy feathers, the kind that come out of a pillow when you whap somebody with it. And because five-year-olds get offended easily, I had to keep being like "Wow, thanks!" and putting them in my pocket. Eventually it dawned on me that unless any eagles or hawks or other humongous birds of prey were swooping into our yard to eat some stale, month-old birdseed, I wasn't going to find a quill-sized feather, so I gave up and went back inside.

That was when I had the idea to borrow one of Dirk the Jerk's stamps instead, for the kind of bonus old-time authenticity that would make Mr. Larrapin dance a dance of sheer and historically accurate delight. A jig, maybe. The two of them would probably be best buds, actually: besides stamp collecting, Dirk the Jerk's main fascination in life is genealogy. He's always bragging about how his family has been in the country since *Mayflower* times, and showing me photocopies of letters from his hallowed innkeeping forbearer Josiah the Jerk, who supposedly knew everybody who was anybody back in Colonial Philadelphia. It's as if he forgets that his ancestors are not my ancestors, which is what you would call extremely ironic, because unless he's waving some piece of fake parchment under my nose, it's not like Dirk the Jerk ever treats me like family. More like I'm some household pest he isn't quite smart enough to get rid of. Although to me, he's the household pest. Or actually, more like some tiny parasite, sitting on my mom's back and slowly draining the fun out of her.

I told Carolyn to go make Mom and Dirk the Jerk play

Go Fish with her, and then I snuck into their bedroom, where he keeps his main stamp book in the bottom drawer of a dresser. I lifted it out: this big dull-red leather-bound thing the size of a baseball base with AMERICAN PHILATELIST SOCIETY stamped on the cover in gold. Stamp dorks should really come up with a name for themselves that doesn't sound so pervy. I creaked it open and started searching for something that looked old enough. I figured that if I was slick, I could just stick it to the envelope really carefully, like with double-sided tape or something, and after the Larrapinball Machine checked it out, I could put it back. No harm, no foul.

Then I remembered what Dirk the Jerk had done a few days earlier at dinner, when Mom was asking me about my day and I was telling her that Claire Wanzandae was my Earth Science lab partner, and that in junior high kids got together and formed study groups to prepare for tests, so maybe I'd occasionally need to go out on a school night, like to Claire's house or something, on the night before a test.

Mom was in the middle of saying that seemed reasonable and asking me what we were studying in Earth Science, when Dirk the Jerk, who was drinking his third beer of the meal, which is about par for the course for him on a

Wednesday night and which is one of the worst things about life with Dirk the Jerk, interrupted. He leaned forward with this weird, cockeyed leer on his face, and said, "Ohhh, yeah. Study group. Bom-chicka-bom-bom-bom." And he made quotation marks around *study group* with his fingers and waggled his eyebrows up and down and tried to nudge my elbow with his, only I moved my elbow out of the way, so he just kind of lurched sideways for no apparent reason.

I felt myself turn bright red, and Mom said, "Dirk..." in her *warning number one* voice. Which is crazy, if you think about it. I mean, if you're my mom and you're using the same voice of authority on your husband as you are on your kids, shouldn't that be like a giant *whoa* sign?

Dirk the Jerk said, "Claire Wanzandae," stretching out all the syllables of her name so it sounded like "Wan... zan...dayyyy," like he was a baseball announcer or some- thing. Then he turned to Carolyn, who was just sitting there, eating her string beans, unaware of how lame her father was being because she's just a sweet, innocent five-year-old, and said, "Hey, Car, I think your brother's got a giiiirlfriend."

Carolyn cocked her head toward him, confused, her pigtails wiggling, and Mom said, "Dirk..." in her *warning number two* voice. And I said, "Shut up, Dirk. You don't know anything." And then Mom said, "Ike…" in her *warning number three* voice, but I was already clearing my plate and walking out of the room, leaving Dirk the Jerk behind me to polish off the final swallow of the bottle and say, "Sheesh, I was only kidding around, sorr-ee," and get up to grab himself another beer.

"Somebody's sensitive," I heard him mumble as I slammed the kitchen door. Dirk the Jerk was definitely either a bully or a kid who got bullied when he was my age; I can't figure out which. But one way or the other, he picked up the tricks of the trade, especially the tactic of pretending everything you've ever done in your life is in the spirit of love and brotherhood right after you ice-pick a person in the heart with words.

I flipped through the stamp book, front to back, using my fingers to bookmark a couple of pages that seemed like they had really ancient ones. When I was satisfied I'd seen them all, I went back and peeled away the cellophane of the page I'd chosen and pressed my thumb against the stamp I wanted, and it came away.

I stared at it for a second, sitting there in my open palm, and thought about how old it was, how somebody had designed and made it a hundred years ago, or maybe two. How that person was dead and gone now, but maybe his great-great-grandkids were somewhere in the world. I thought about how this stamp had been made to go on an envelope but in all that time it had never achieved its purpose, never been used for the one single thing its maker had intended. Then I thought, *Screw you, Dirk, you deserve it,* and turned it over and gave it a big old, juicy lick and stuck it right onto the corner of the envelope.

# CHAPTER 3

Sometimes the cafeteria of life is sold out of everything but poopburgers. And sometimes the circumstances of the moment won't allow you to say, "Oh, you know what? I'm actually not that hungry." Sometimes you've got to step right up to the counter and order a double poopburger with a side of tater snots and a nice, tall glass of ice-cold badger vomit.

Guess what we did in history class that Monday as a big, fun surprise, seeing as almost everybody did the extra credit after getting smacked down by Larrapin's first test, which was all essay and so long that nobody even finished it, and during which he spent the whole time pacing up and down the aisles like some kind of evil cyborg named Distractotron 4000, with a big smile on his face like the best thing in the whole world is watching a room full of kids get muscle cramps in their writing hands?

The answer is, we read our letters to famous historical figures out loud. Correction: Mr. Larrapin read them out loud.

Obviously there was no way I could let him read mine, since it called him an unflattering name and also contained personal information about myself and other people—especially Claire Wanzandae, who is also in Honors History and in fact sits directly in front of me, with her long, glossy black hair that smells like a combination of orange blossoms and gasoline, hanging over the back of her chair, so close that I could comb it for her.

But Mr. Larrapin, sneaky weasel that he is, began class by saying, "So, who did the extra-credit assignment?" and I raised my hand and put my letter on my desk, thinking he was just going to go around and check off names, the way he had when the extra credit was to make a blueprint of a British theater. A lot of the nerdier kids were pretty mad when he only took one nanosecond to look at each blueprint, when they'd probably spent all weekend hard at work with their slide rules or whatever. But the craftier kids, myself included, were like, "Aha, extra credit is a joke to Mr.

HUGE pain in my ▓▓▓▓!

Larrapin, even though it's worth up to five points on your test grade." Which was a much-needed chink in the armor of his class, because for the most part Mr. Larrapin grades like we're a bunch of PhD candidates or something.

So anyway, he said, "Let's read a few, shall we?" as if he'd just thought of it, and started walking down the first row of desks, which is mine. Claire handed him her letter, which I could see was written in her perfect, girly cursive and began with *Dear Marie Antoinette* and wasn't in an envelope or anything. And then Mr. Larrapin was hovering over me.

"Franklin?" he said, and for a second I thought he was saying my name, and I wanted to punch him in the face. Then I saw that he was looking at the envelope, with BF's name and the Philadelphia street address I'd found for him on the Internet written on it in smudgy, pseudo-old-timey, looped script.

"Interesting choice," he said, holding out his hand.

"I didn't know anybody was going to read them," I said, and covered the letter with my fist. "Mine is kind of personal. And I already sealed it. With wax." I showed him the wax, which came out not great, because I had to use a sea-foam-scented bath candle of my mom's, but it still showed Effort.

Mr. Larrapin got this soft look in his eyes when I said it, as if he realized that this was an embarrassing situation to be in if you were me, and he didn't want to make it worse.

"I see," he said, and for a second, I started to really like him. But then, even though his heart was in the right place, he made a totally boneheaded decision, which was to look around at the class and say, "Did anybody else write a letter that's too personal to read?"

Mr. Larrapin probably believed he was getting me off the hook, or else he was realizing he should have thought of this earlier, and maybe he ought to cancel this activity before it backfired in his face, because who knows what was in these letters? But what he was doing in reality was (a) threatening the class with actual work when it had already geared up for something fun and time-wasting and nontestable, and (b) giving anybody who felt like making fun of me a perfect opening, by asking a question that any twelve-year-old basically hears as "Is anybody else as big a loser as Ike?" Also, (c) he was making it all my fault if (a) happened.

So of course, everybody shouted in unison, "No!" and then a couple of kids, for good measure, added stuff like, "What did you tell him, Ike? Who you have a crush on?" and "Read Ike's!" So even though the crisis of having my letter read out loud got averted, I still looked like a creepy weirdo, and of course I turned bright red to top it off. And then Mr. Larrapin, who knew he should say something but obviously had no idea what, turned back to me and went, "Half credit," before moving down the row.

Also unfortunate about this situation was that History was the last class of the day, so when the period ended, everybody was slap-happy from a rare fun class—which in addition to The Humiliation of Franklin Isaac Saturday included such highlights as Matty Hall's letter to Thomas Crapper, who might or might not have invented the toilet, and Christine Macabe's letter to Michael Jackson, who she claimed was a historical figure because he was dead.

So everybody walked out of the room in the mood to blow off even more steam, which took the form of Dan McCarthy and Mark Giroux deciding they were going to get their hands on my letter and read it. They followed me through the hall and then out of the building, saying, "C'mon, dude. Show us the letter," over and over, the way Carolyn does to our mom when she wants a cookie or something.

"You guys sound like my little sister," I said. I didn't know what I thought this would accomplish, but then again, I didn't really know what they were trying to accomplish, either. I barely knew Dan and Mark, so why did they care what I'd written? The answer was probably that they were just hassling me for the fun of it. Which is another one of those things I understand but don't.

I do know that both Mark and Dan were on the Cool Bros list for that party, so now they're pals or pseudo-pals with Ryan, and as they followed me down the broad front steps of the school and onto the street, where the buses pulled up, I looked around hoping he'd appear and tell them to chill out. Or at least say "what's up" to me, which would also have caused them to back off.

"What did you tell Ben Franklin, dude? That you're gay?" Mark Giroux said, and both of them laughed. Half the school was coming outside now to wait for their buses, everybody who didn't have an after-school activity or live close enough to walk. This meant that Dan and Mark had an audience to show off for. It also meant that if I could play it cool enough, they might end up being the ones who looked stupid. So right away, I decided that this was my strategy: act bored by the whole thing, like they really were five-year-olds.

"'Dear Ben Franklin,'" Dan McCarthy said, pretending to write on his hand with an invisible pen. "'You are the only one who understands how hard it is to be a massive gaylord who's never kissed a girl.'"

I realize I should have probably just ignored it, but what Dan was saying was so mean and stupid that I couldn't resist taking the bait.

"If I *were* gay," I said, "why would I want to kiss a girl?"

Neither one of them had a ready answer for that, and now everybody at the bus stop was paying total attention because this was starting to get interesting. *Maybe there will be a fight,* they were thinking.

"So you're saying you're gay?" Mark Giroux said.

"No," I said. "But what if I was? Are you saying you have something against gay people?"

"No," said Mark. "Of course not. I just—" But it was a trick, because at that moment he stopped talking, whipped his arm around my back super fast, and snatched the envelope out of my back pocket.

"Let's get to the bottom of this, shall we?" he said, and flipped it around.

This was very not good, especially because Claire Wanzandae was now walking toward the bus stop, her hair swinging back and forth behind her like life was one big shampoo commercial.

I lunged for the envelope, but Mark pulled it out of reach.

"Don't be a jerk," I said. "Give it back."

"Who's gonna make him?" Dan said, and stepped between me and Mark so I couldn't even see what he was doing, much less get to him.

"Give it back," I said again, and by now I wanted to cry and almost was crying. That would be the end of me, of course. I'd have to convince my mother to send me to private school or something.

"Why are you guys acting like such idiots?" I heard. And out of nowhere, standing right next to me, was Claire Wanzandae with her arms crossed in front of her chest. Mark and Dan both stopped what they were doing and stared at her.

"Give him back his letter," she said. "What the hell?"

"You gonna let your girlfriend fight your battles for you, dude?" asked Dan.

Weirdly, just hearing him call Claire my girlfriend was incredibly thrilling, and suddenly I didn't know if my heart was racing from fear or from excitement.

"I thought I was gay," I said like a total moron, and stifled the urge to slap myself in the forehead.

HUGE pain in my ████████!

Dan opened his mouth to respond. Meanwhile, Mark went back to work on the letter, trying to dislodge the huge glob of wax I'd dripped on there. Before he could get anywhere, though, Claire reached over and snatched it out of his hand as if he actually were a five-year-old.

"Hey!" he said like a goon, and looked up. But Claire was already walking away—from them and from the bus stop and from me.

I ran after her even though my bus had just pulled up and I'd have no way to get home if I missed it, unless I felt like walking about six miles. What else could I do, though?

I was breathing hard by the time I caught up. Claire has incredibly long legs, like a giraffe or a flamingo or something. She's a head and a half taller than me—and taller than Mark and Dan, too, for that matter. She's basically a giant. A very cute giant.

"Hey," I panted. And then I ran out of other stuff to say.

Claire handed me the letter without breaking her stride. The seal was still intact. Just then the wind shifted in our direction, and the aroma of sea-foam candle hit me in the face.

"Thanks," I said. "You're like a superhero or something."

Claire made a little snorty laugh sound through her nose, like a small, adorable horse would do.

"No, really," I said. "I mean, you saved the day. Mark and Dan would probably be dead by now, if you hadn't shown up. Guts spread all over the pavement. And I'd be looking at life in prison, or the electric chair."

She opened her mouth and laughed a different laugh, more trilly, like a giant, pretty bird. All of a sudden, I was feeling really good about myself, despite all the torture of the past two hours. It was like Claire brought out the smartness in me. I felt loose and entertaining, like I could have jumped onstage at a comedy club and knocked the crowd's socks off. It's a feeling I don't get that often. Maybe once in a while, when I'm making my mom laugh, which is usually when Dirk the Jerk is away on some stupid work trip and it's just the two of us.

"Ben Franklin, huh?" Claire Wanzandae said.

"Yeah," I said. "I'm named after him, so I figure the least he can do is listen to me complain."

She gave me a sideways smile of, like, encouragement. As if Claire Wanzandae was saying, *Keep going, Ike. You're killing it right now.*

That was when I saw the mailbox on the corner, and a great idea popped into my head. And as we walked past, I opened the slot and slipped the letter inside, real casual, still talking to Claire as I did it, like the whole thing was no big deal and I was mailing a phone bill for my mom or something.

She thought it was freaking hilarious. SCORE. I ended up walking her all the way to her house, like ten blocks, by which time I'd found out a ton of stuff about her, including that we both think Mr. Larrapin is a toolbox, both like the same cheesy nineties action movies, and both are worried that Earth Science is going to keep us off honor roll. In other words, we have EVERYTHING in common and are basically soul mates. I didn't exactly ask her out, but I totally could have. I barely noticed the six-mile walk home, and I certainly didn't give any thought to mailing the letter, except to pat myself on the back for executing such a smooth move, one I'll probably be telling our grandkids about someday in the distant future, after Claire and I get married and grow old together.

# CHAPTER 4

Philad. April 17, 1776

Dear Franklin,

I received your letter of April 5 and found your Impudence to be repugnant and provoking. That a young man bereft of even the most basic knowledge as to what year this is should address a Founding Father, statesman, inventor, printer, author, politician, scientist, musician, philosopher, and creator of the Very postal system that delivered your rather vile missive infused me with a disdain reminiscent of that I directed at King George III after his issuance of the Stamp Act.

HUGE pain in my ▓▓▓!

Therefore, in my fervent desire to terminate this correspondence with swift dispatch, I conclude with the bold proclamation that I have earned the right to merrily capitalize whichever letters I please and that it is My most modest assumption That a scamp such as yourself would experience overwhelming difficulty negotiating even life's most rudimentary situations no matter what your first name Was.

I am,
Benjamin Franklin

# CHAPTER 5

I only really get mail on my birthday, from my grandma. She's always good for a Garfield card with a ten-dollar bill inside, so crispy it's like she ironed it. Why Garfield, which is basically the most boring comic strip ever, I have no idea. Maybe my mom was a fan when she was little or something, back when times were simpler, and it got frozen in Grandma's head that Kids = Love of Garfield.

Even old people have pretty much given up on the U.S. Postal Service, though. My grandma mostly Skypes us when she wants to talk, although she's really bad at getting the camera to work, or knowing where to look when she does get it turned on, and she's always blaming her computer and calling it defective, which is funny at first and then extremely tiresome.

Despite never getting any mail, I always check the mailbox. Back when my dad still lived with us, he used to get these cool car catalogs from companies like Lamborghini and Porsche, which he'd somehow convinced that he was in the market for a luxury automobile even though he drove a Honda Civic that, if you removed the air freshener, would've lost half its value. The catalogs always came with little gifts, like soft cloths called shammies that you were supposed to use to wipe all the dead bugs off the windshield of the car you hadn't bought yet, on account of killing so many by slamming into them at 160 miles per hour all the time.

Now my dad lives in California, and for all I know he drives some cool bug-smashing car. I basically only see him a few times a year, when he comes back here and stays at his buddy Dave's place, which he is always apologizing for and saying stuff like *It breaks my heart, Ikey* when we're talking on the phone. Which also only happens about once every two weeks even though in theory it's supposed to be every few days, but we both forget a lot, me because I have school and other responsibilities to think about and him because his hours at work are always switching and getting unexpectedly extended and stuff. Nobody calls me Ikey anymore but Carolyn, but I guess he still mostly thinks of me as being a little kid. I want to ask him why he moved across the country if it's so heartbreaking, and also why he says it like it's my fault, or something that both of us decided on together and have to regret together every time we talk. But I don't, because I don't want to make him sadder when he seems to be pretty sad already. Plus, I know he'd say he had to go where the work was, and there was no work here, and how he had this one-in-a-million chance to get in some fancy union for carpenters who build movie sets or something, which I can tell he wants me to be all impressed by. But really, what's the difference between hammering nails into a house or a fake pirate ship, besides that one of them has to be done three thousand miles away from your only kid?

But anyway, checking the mail together was one of our little father-and-son activities, and I still do it, out of habit and missing him. Which mostly means doing Dirk the Jerk the favor of bringing his stupid stamp-collector magazines inside, along with the usual bills and full-color grocery-store circulars advertising thirty-five cents off foods we don't eat anyway. Also clothing catalogs, which were my main reason for getting the mail until recently, because

I'd shown Carolyn how to draw mustaches and horns on people, and for a while we were really into that. But then she had one of those random moral awakenings five-year-olds are always going through and decided that drawing on people "is not very nice." Nothing makes you feel like more of a winner than having your little sister inform you that she's too mature now for the game you taught her, let me tell you. Good times.

It was Friday when the letter came. Mom and Dirk the Jerk were still at work, and Carolyn was at the After-School Program, which I taught her to call the After-School Slow Jam, like Slow Jam Saturdays on 98.7 WFKO. I thought that was pretty funny, but Teacher Lucinda didn't appreciate it. Teacher Lucinda had been my after-school teacher too, back in the day, when she was still married and called herself Mrs. Carp. I bet she would have laughed about it then.

My first thought when I saw a letter addressed to me in big black cursive script was that it was junk mail, which I sometimes get, who knows why. That's one of the junk mail companies' tricks: to make it look like somebody took the time to write out the words all fancy, so that you open the envelope. At which point you realize it's just the American Acronym Association asking for donations or whatever.

I opened it anyway, because why not, and that's when I got mad. My letter to Ben Franklin had blown over by then, or so I'd thought. Giroux and McCarthy hadn't said a word about it the next day, maybe figuring the whole episode was a net loss for them. And I'd put it out of my mind and moved on to other things, like figuring out what time the after-sports buses came and whether I could take one and still beat Mom back to our house, since that way I could walk Claire Wanzandae home again. She and I had gotten super chatty and even started walking from Earth Science to History together, in full view of everybody. And those classes are on opposite sides of the building, so I was guaranteed at least five minutes a day with her, and I'd been pretty consistently making her laugh. Twice so hard that she touched my arm, which is like Dork First Base basically.

I had a bunch of thoughts all at once when I read the letter, all of them the bad kind that make your stomach flip around like you might puke. One was that Giroux and McCarthy had somehow followed me and Claire that day and gotten my letter out of the mailbox after we walked past.

That seemed kind of unlikely, though, since (a) everybody knows you can't get into a mailbox, because it's Federal and made of solid metal, and the whole country would pretty much collapse if stealing letters was something any random goober could accomplish on a moment's notice, and (b) if they had gotten into it, there was plenty more incriminating stuff in the letter that they could have chosen to focus on besides my name and that thing about capitalizing letters. Also (c) it wasn't their style to write a fake letter from Ben Franklin as a means of screwing with my mind. They were more the type to just put my letter up on Facebook for everyone to read and pass around and laugh at, and (d) even if they did decide to do a letter, those two goons wouldn't have bothered to find a quill and ink and weird, crinkly thin paper, or pick the right old-timey words to make the letter seem real. Or find an old-timey stamp identical to the one I'd taken from Dirk the Jerk, which this letter had.

All that meant I had to consider other possibilities, such as: Claire Wanzandae had written the letter as some kind of bizarro inside joke. She wouldn't have had to jimmy open the mailbox, because I'd told her what my letter said—the part about my name, anyway, and maybe the Capitalization stuff, too. I couldn't remember. Also, Claire was smart enough to pull off a letter like this, with all the extra old-timey flourishes, and she was weird enough, too, in a good way.

And as an extra added bonus, if she'd spent all that time creating an elaborately fake letter, she had to like me, for real. The more I thought about it, the more I decided Ben Franklin was Claire Wanzandae, and this was her adorable, nut-ball way of flirting—especially since I had no other suspects whatsoever. So by dinnertime, my anger had one hundred percent evaporated, replaced by a warm, jangly feeling of excitement as I thought about what my next move should be.

# CHAPTER 6

I waited until after Earth Science to say anything, even though we had a lab day and spent the whole period identifying igneous and sedimentary rocks from slides, which meant plenty of standing close to each other and catching whiffs of Claire's hair and also the medicine cream she uses on the backs of her hands to prevent outbreaks of eczema, which she's had since third grade. In fifth, it got so bad that she scratched her hands bloody in the middle of a chorus concert and had to wear white cotton gloves for a week afterward, but then her parents took her to a really nice dermatologist, and since then it's been under control. This is the type of highly personal stuff I am beginning to learn about Claire Wanzandae, which is important for Trust. Without Trust, you don't have a foundation for a relationship.

After class we started walking toward History, which means crossing the breezeway. This is a kind of outdoor hallway that connects the two school buildings, and for some reason it's where you go to make out, I guess because it's .0001 percent more private than a regular hallway. It's also where Trevor Koppelman got busted smoking a cigarette last week by Doug Rotatelli, the boys' lacrosse coach and school disciplinarian, who basically walks around all day with a lacrosse stick, fighting crime or whatever. He is considered "cool" by kids like Ryan, because he doesn't do anything if he catches you smooching a girl, even though that's just as much against the rules as smoking. Doug Rotatelli was probably part of the popular crowd in junior high, which ought to say something about how valuable that is, long term.

"So," I told Claire as we stepped outside into the breezeway breeze, "I got a very interesting letter yesterday."

"Oh yeah?" she said. "I never get mail, except from my grandparents."

I looked at her real sharply, but nothing about her face or the way she said it was smirky, like a person trying to hold a secret in her mouth.

I must have spaced out looking at her, because Claire said, "So? Who was it from, already?"

HUGE pain in my ▓▓▓▓▓!

I took the envelope out of my back pocket and said, "Come on. You know."

Claire shrugged her hair back over one shoulder and then the other, which is a thing she does, and said, "You're being weird, Ike."

I felt my hand start sweating onto the paper. Partly because she genuinely seemed to have no idea what I was talking about and partly because that was what happened anytime she said my name.

"You're telling me you didn't write this?" I asked, and handed it to her.

Claire Wanzandae turned the envelope over in her hands, examining both sides. She ran her thumb over the stamp, picked at the broken, dried blood-color wax seal with a fingernail painted in glossy see-through nail polish, even lifted the whole thing to her nose and inhaled. All that before reaching inside and unfolding the letter.

Kids had been streaming past us the whole time on their way to class, but now the traffic had slowed to a trickle. Any second, the bell would ring and we'd be late to History. Claire didn't look like she cared. A deep line appeared on her face, slashing from her forehead to the bridge of her nose, as she read the letter. By the time she looked up, the breezeway was deserted and the bell had come and gone.

"Why would you think I wrote this?" she asked, still frowning.

"I dunno," I said. "Like, as a joke? You're the only one who knew what my letter said, so I thought…"

"This stamp is super old," she informed me, and for a second I got angry, like, *Come on, Claire Wanzandae, don't you think I noticed that?*

"I know," I said in a dead-fish voice like Mom uses when Dirk the Jerk lectures her about money after three beers while eating one of Carolyn's child-sized soy chocolate puddings.

"I mean, where would I get a stamp like that, even if I did want to…" Claire crossed her arms over her chest, and cocked her head at me like a puppy that can't figure out why you're telling it to come inside. "Want to *what*, exactly?"

By then I was done being mad and had moved on to fretting that I'd blown it with Claire by acting like a crazy person. I felt like an air mattress with its valve open and a bunch of kids jumping up and down on its stomach.

"Hello? Earth to Ike." Claire waved the letter in front of my face.

"Sorry," I mumbled. "What did you say?"

"I said, so who did? Because it definitely wasn't me. I don't even know what 'repugnant' means."

"It's like disgusting," I told her, and a cold, clammy feeling came over me. Like I was being watched. Or like something bad was waiting for me just around the corner, and there was nothing I could do, because I didn't know which corner.

"Somebody's messing with me," I said, and hearing the words hit the air only made the feeling creep up higher inside, like water rising in a flooding basement. "Somebody's messing with me in a major way. And I have no idea who. Or why. Or how."

That was when Claire took my hand and interlaced her fingers with mine. "Don't worry," she said. "We'll figure it out." And by "we," Claire Wanzandae meant her and me. We had become a we somehow. The water stopped rising inside me when she said it, but it still reached right up to my neck.

# CHAPTER 7

The next day, Claire Wanzandae was AT MY HOUSE. It just kind of happened, like it was no big deal, even though I'd shown up at Earth Science with the specific purpose of taking our relationship to the next level by casually mentioning a screening of *Die Hard 2* that was coming up in two weeks on Throwback Thursday at the other, less popular movie theater in town, the one with only two screens and seats that don't even have drink holders attached.

I'd psyched myself up by drinking half of Mom's coffee when she wasn't looking, so that I'd be full of energy and also laser-focused on my mission of suaveness. But by the time Mrs. Broussard stopped lecturing and let us go back to the microscopes, I was feeling a lot less powerful and dynamic than I'd anticipated, and a lot more like I might have a brain aneurysm from the effort of not ripping a fart the size of a hot air balloon.

Claire took one glance at me and knew something was wrong, though luckily she didn't know what. "You look exhausted," she whispered as we sorted our stupid tray of slides from 1979. "You were up worrying about the letter, weren't you?"

I nodded my head, because who knew what would happen if I opened my mouth. Something very disgusting, possibly.

"I knew it," Claire said, sounding weirdly satisfied. "I woke up at, like, one in the morning, thinking about it. I almost called, but I figured your mom would kill me."

Thinking about my mom and Claire in the same sentence was sort of unsettling for some reason, though obviously in the distant future when Claire was the mother of her grand-children, they'd be spending a lot of time together.

"You figured right," I said out of the corner of my mouth, so that Mrs. Broussard, whose pet peeve is anybody talking about non–Earth Science stuff during a lab, wouldn't come over and shake her turkey neck at us. "Listen, I'll be right back. I left my pen in my locker."

"You can borrow—" Claire said, reaching into her back-pack, but I'd already darted for the door. I closed it behind me and let loose an Extinction Level Event at the exact moment Mark Giroux stepped into the corridor from the next classroom down.

I froze in embarrassment as the smell rose up around me and galloped down the hall.

"Holy crap, Saturday," Mark said, crinkling up his nose. "Nice one."

"Thanks," I said, and waited for whatever horrible thing was going to happen next.

But instead, Mark just said, "Catch you later, dude," and walked off toward the bathroom.

I'm telling you, I do not understand one freaking thing about junior high school.

I was still reeling from the encounter and wondering if me and Mark Giroux had somehow become bros, and if so when and how, or was he maybe just a big fan of flatulence, when I went back inside.

"So," Claire Wanzandae said, picking up right where she'd left off, "the first thing we've got to do is examine all the evidence."

"Uh-huh," I agreed, totally distracted because on second thought maybe it was all a trick and I was going to walk out of class and find Giroux and McCarthy and a hundred other kids pointing and laughing and making fart noises at me. Anything was possible. Heck, some creep was mailing me fake Ben Franklin letters. My life was like a helicopter smashing into a train wreck.

"I'll come over today, and we'll get to the bottom of it," she declared.

My brain didn't quite process that. Claire blinked her pretty eyes at me, maybe hoping the breeze from her eyelids would snap me out of my coma. "If you want me to, I mean."

"No," I said. "I mean, yes. Absolutely. Great. My parents don't get home until five thirty, so we'll have the place to ourselves. So we can work without distractions, I mean. On solving the, you know, the thing."

"Good," said Claire, and I spent the rest of Earth Science, and every class after Earth Science, wondering which part she meant was good. Like, were we going to work on solving the thing, or was that just an excuse? Was this a date? Was there anything embarrassing at home that I should rush inside and hide? I still had a couple of stuffed animals in my room, for instance—just for old times' sake, not because I played with them. But I could always blame them on Carolyn, if she asked. Also, my dental retainer was almost definitely sitting on my nightstand, looking like a big pink wad of spat-out Big League Chew with wires stuck in it, not exactly the kind of thing to put Claire Wanzandae in the mood for romance. And all that was if we even got to my bedroom at all. Maybe we were going to sit at the kitchen table with magnifying glasses and Sherlock Holmes hats. Maybe she just felt sorry for me, or liked playing amateur detective.

When school let out, we got on my bus together. Ryan wasn't there to see it, because he had lacrosse practice, but plenty of kids definitely took notice. It made me feel good to be seen with Claire, and I played it up a little bit for the benefit of whoever cared, touching the small of her back with my hand and guiding her into a seat and stuff. I guess I was pretending she was my girlfriend, which maybe sounds a little weird or creepy, but I wasn't doing it to fool anybody. More like to try it on for size, to see how it fit.

It's funny how seeing old stuff with a new person makes everything look fresh, and at the same time it brings out all kinds of memories. I found myself pointing out these personal landmarks to Claire as we got off the highway and rolled through my neighborhood, as if this trip to my house was really a trip through my childhood: "There's the grocery store I used to walk to with my dad for Popsicles when I was little." "This block is where my friend Ryan tried to do a wheelie on his bike and broke his front tooth when we were nine." "That's my old elementary school. See the map of the U.S. painted on the blacktop outside? My third-grade class did that. I got to color Arkansas." None of it was super-fascinating stuff, but so what, because that stuff was my life, and you're allowed to tell a girl about your life, even if it isn't all snake pits and daring jailbreaks.

We got off the bus a stop early, because (a) I figured I'm better on my feet than sitting down, in terms of being funny and getting Claire Wanzandae in the right frame of mind to look at this afternoon as the beginning of her new life as my girlfriend, and (b) I wanted to avoid getting off at the same stop as my old nemesis Amanda "Bony" Loanie, who lives at the top of my block and whose mom is friends with my mom, so we always used to get thrown together on playdates and stuff when we were little kids, only we never got along and Amanda is a busybody like her mother, and if she saw me walking into my house with Claire, it was a safe bet that my mom would hear about it within ten nano-seconds. Me having a girl over with nobody home wasn't forbidden, exactly, but it was definitely a legal gray area and nothing Mom or Dirk the Jerk needed to know about at this particular juncture, especially with so much still up in the air regarding me and Claire Wanzandae's future.

So we took the long way, and sure enough, I was able to crack a couple of good ones, including an impression of Mrs. Broussard foraging for worms that made Claire giggle into her hand in this amazing way she had. By my count, she had four different laughs, and that was the second-best one. So things were off to a pretty rad start, and honestly I wasn't even really thinking about the Franklin letter, and the queasy feeling of being watched that had filled me up when I first read it had pretty much faded away.

Then we got to my house, and out of habit, I checked the mailbox.

# CHAPTER 8

June 11, 1776

Dear Franklin—

Jungle Juice?
I believe that was the name you assigned to the saucy medley concocted by the union of trace amounts of liquor procured from numerous bottles to elude detection of usage. And if by chance my recollection is in error, I attribute my current clouded condition to the rather potent brew that I, Benjamin Franklin, printer by trade, diplomat by fame, and man of action by all accounts, just concocted and Imbibed in this Pennsylvania State House library, to which I have

momentarily retreated before I rejoin the others In the chamber with which this room shares a common wall to parse the wording Of what will soon become known as the colonies' Declaration of Independence.

What prompts this outreach to a young letter writer with whom I heretofore wanted no part of is a kindred feeling of Isolation. Disenfranchisement. Within your realm, at the hands of Allie, Jennifer, and Melissa, who have decreed you to be socially anathema, while the names of my oppressors are the honorable Mssrs. John Adams of Massachusetts, Robert Sherman of Connecticut, and Robert Livingston of New York—all three of whom concur that Thomas Jefferson of Virginia should draft the aforementioned document because he possesses the best handwriting.

For this I returned with requested dispatch from my long-awaited vacation Abroad? For sycophantic subordination to a slave owner with a multitude of unaccounted-for progeny who is now the object of exultation by dint of penmanship? To become a footnoted member of a "Committee of Five"? To merely advise a bully whose inflated delusions of entitlement extend to the brazen appropriation of the hitching post closest to the front door of this noble edifice, a hitching post that was designated for yours truly in deference to my advanced years and acutely bowed lower body?

Granted, I am not a classically handsome man. Providence, for reasons all its own, saw fit to bestow me with more than ample girth in areas where less would have sufficed, and a dearth in others, rendering them spindly at best. However, most disturbing is the matter of my hair—as what I am in need of, in general, is more.

Though of the variety I do possess, I would have preferred less. Or none at all. Or Thomas Jefferson's.

Yet, I have courted a greater amount of fair maidens than the expected allotment for a man of my physical deficiencies. Attributable, with no doubt, to the cultivation of traits situated beyond the scope of empirical inspection and evaluation. To wit, wit. And a propensity for arranging words in an axiomatic order that will elicit a nod in response to their profundity. "Early to bed, and early to rise, makes a man healthy, wealthy, and wise" and "Love thy neighbor, but don't pull down your hedge" are but two examples. Despite your severely wrongheaded claim, I never uttered, "A stitch in time saves nine," although I do imagine that I will eventually declare that "A stench in the sun is never fun" if my dream of founding a Philadelphia Zoo is ever realized.

I am, by nature, a modest soul presently comporting with uncharacteristic bravado for the singular purpose of demonstrating a lifelong credo that no impediment is insurmountable and no challenge too...no challenge too...Lord, this Jungle Juice is a rather jaunty mix...no challenge too...did I mention that I'm not a classically handsome man?

I must now take leave to begrudgingly rejoin the Committee chosen to scribe the document that will announce and Explain the reasons for our desired separation from our mother country. Soon, all literate citizens of our thirteen colonies shall be reading it with manifest Pride and Resolve, in myriad newspapers great and small.

And I offer you my solemn word, young Franklin, that if Mssrs. John Adams of Massachusetts, Robert Sherman of Connecticut, Robert Livingston of New York, and You-Know-Who from Virginia manifest the same disrespect with which your peers are shunning you, they will leave me no option but to snatch the parchment and set it aflame by directing the sun's light upon it through a pair of bifocals, which I also invented.

I am (not a classically handsome man),
Benjamin Franklin

# CHAPTER 9

We read it together, right in my driveway. Afterward, Claire and I just stood there, staring down at the pages in my hand. I didn't want to be the first one to open my mouth and say something totally bonkers, and I guess she didn't, either, so we just stood there forever.

That's what it felt like, anyway. In reality, it was probably only about ninety seconds before Claire Wanzandae touched three cool, dry fingers to my arm and said "Ike" in a low voice. I raised my eyes to hers and saw that her slinky black eyebrows were lifted so high they'd disappeared into her bangs.

"This is going to sound crazy," she said, "but I think this letter really is from Benjamin Franklin." She looked away, and rolled a pebble with her foot.

"You're right," I said. "That's totally insane. Ben Franklin died in…" I realized I had no idea when BF had bought the farm. "In times of yore." I shuffled the pages and looked at the first line again.

"*Somebody* got my letter, though," I said. "I talked about Jungle Juice in there. This is too freaking weird."

"Check out the stamp," Claire said, grabbing the envelope. "It's super old. Just like the last one."

"And the one on my letter," I said, and something clicked for both of us at the same time, which sometimes happens when you're soul mates.

"Why would the post office—"

"Deliver three letters with two-cent stamps?"

"Exactly. I mean, they're worth a lot more than that in real life—like, to stamp collectors."

"Not once you lick them, they're not," Claire said. "Then, they're ruined."

We both pondered that for a minute. Claire looked super serious, and I tried to match her level of intensity even though I was mostly reflecting that things were headed down Thomas Crapper's glorious invention, as far as the chances of us locking lips on the living room couch like I'd been planning, which I now put at 23 percent likely, down 57 percent from an hour earlier.

"Here's what we do," Claire said suddenly, and a little flush came into her cheeks. "We send another letter and see what happens. Can you get another stamp as old as this?"

"Sure," I said. "Dirk the Jerk has plenty." Claire shot me a look. "My stepfather," I explained. "He's a philatelist."

Claire's eyes widened to the size of Frisbees. "Is he registered?"

"It means stamp dork."

"Oh."

"So what's this letter supposed to say?" I asked. "Maybe we should demand that he prove he's Ben Franklin and see what happens. Like, we could ask him to send us, I dunno, some scrimshaw or something. They were into scrimshaw back then, I'm pretty sure." I sounded like a moron, even to myself. I didn't even know what scrimshaw was. "Or, hey, a copy of the newspaper—that would be good, right? That's what they make hostages hold, to prove what date it is. And it's not like the guy who wrote us this letter can just come up with a newspaper from 1776, right?"

Claire shook her head. "I don't think we should push him. What did you say in your first letter? You just told him about your life, right?"

"Yeah, pretty much. And insulted him a bunch."

"So do that again. And ask him some questions. About that thing with Jefferson, maybe. He seems pretty upset about that."

I was starting to get the feeling that Claire and I weren't totally on the same page.

"Um, Claire…you do realize it's not really Ben Franklin who wrote this, right? It's just some guy playing a joke on me."

"Maybe," she said kind of distantly.

"Because…that would be impossible," I said, looking right up into her clear brown eyes.

"Nothing's impossible," she said very firmly, sounding like some weird combination of a grown-up and a little kid.

I was going to object, but right then Claire Wanzandae leaned forward and kissed me on the lips. Which seemed like proof that maybe she was right.

# CHAPTER 10

April 15, 2015

Dear Ben,

First of all, thanks for writing me Back, even if you were Drunk when you did it. Slurping down Jungle Juice and writing letters—man, you sure are living the Dream.

Second of all, I'm sorry for being kind of a jerk before. I guess I was taking out my Frustrations with Life on you, which isn't fair since none of it is your Fault, really. So I take back calling you a stringy-haired old windbag, which was a totally lame move on my part. I didn't know how sensitive you are about your hair, and besides, I didn't really Expect you to read my letter anyway. Have you tried using conditioner? Maybe you don't have conditioner over there in 1776, but it's this product that's supposed to give your hair more "luster and body," according to the bottle my mom uses. And hey, if conditioner doesn't exist, maybe I can send you a list of ingredients and you can Invent it, and add that to your very impressive list of Accomplishments to Brag about in Letters.

Anyway, you'll be glad to hear that things are Better with me. Or maybe you won't be glad, since the only reason you stopped dissing me and wrote that second letter was out of sympathy for how Isolated we both are in our Realms. But check it out: Claire Wanzandae and I are basically a couple now, and you're partly responsible because your letter helped bring us together. So I'm very Grateful, and anything I can do to help you Screw Over Jefferson and the rest of those clowns, just let me know.

In fact, I did a little research for you already, by Googling "JOHN ADAMS SCANDAL," and apparently that dude has practically Never kissed a female human being in his life, according to Esquire magazine, which also went so far as to describe him as "practically a eunuch." Plus, his son Charles is going to drink himself to death in 1800.

I can't see how either of those facts could be of use, but there they are just in Case. As for Jefferson, you already know about that Sally Hemings stuff, but guess what Else? He's going to have an affair with Dolley Madison sometime around 1812, according to Salon.com, and it may or may not be a reason for the War. So maybe you can Nail him for that, if you're not too busy chasing all kinds of ladies around Paris, which according to that same article you are pretty Famous for, disgusting hair or not.

Anyway, the thing I'm worried about now is, how do you keep a girl like Claire Wanzandae happy? I mean, look, Ben Franklin: She's taller than me, she's mega-beautiful, she takes all honors classes, and she's funny. Any guy would be lucky to get her, and I guess what I'm worried about is that my luck is going to run Out, because I pretty much am just Any Guy. I mean, I know you said that Wit is how you impress the ladies, but keep in mind that you're also basically an American Icon, and probably the Ladies of your Realm are more into clever little turns of phrase than the ones here, who mostly care more about how a guy's arms look, even if he is cracking them up all the time, because a Friend can also do that. Let's be honest: Right now, the most interesting thing I've got going on is that I get letters from You. No Offense, but how pathetic is that?

You'll probably say I should stop seeing the glass as half empty instead of half full—or, to be more Accurate, that I should stop worrying that the Glass, which is full of a Delicious Beverage, is going to be empty some Time in the future. Maybe you made up that expression, for all I know. If so, bully for You.

Sorry, Ben Franklin. I'm just ranting again, and I'm not even drunk like you. Please write back and tell me what I should do to keep things Exciting for Claire. The truth is, I don't really have anyone else to ask. Ryan would just say some dumb macho junk about never letting a girl get inside your head, my dad barely answers his phone most of the time, and I'd rather stick a Wilkinson Sword into my own eyeball than talk about Guy Stuff with Dirk the Jerk.

Also, seriously, let me know if there is anything I can do to Help with your Situation, like maybe by providing Information, because let's just say I have Access to a large Web of that. And besides, getting drunk is no solution to your problems, Ben Franklin, and neither is setting the Declaration of Independence on fire.

Finally, let me ask you one more thing: If it's not too much trouble, could you enclose a few stamps with your next letter? I have almost run out and they are hard to come by here in my Realm, believe it or not. And while I Apologize for asking, I figured it would be less Rude than just leaving you Hanging because of No Stamps.

Your friend,
F. I. Saturday

# CHAPTER 11

Dirk the Jerk's annual company dinner was that Thursday at some fancy hotel in the city. That meant I was babysitting Carolyn, which was supposedly a big deal because I'd never done it before—except of course for all the millions of times I'd done it before. But in Mom's mind those didn't count because they were during the day, when all the big, gruesome monsters are asleep. She spent the whole last hour before she left barking instructions at me, as if I were a dimwitted stranger who had never met Carolyn or been inside a house before. Stuff like "She can have one Popsicle, Ike. No more," and "Remember, if you need anything, the Freedmans are right across the street," plus special bonus pearls of wisdom like "Don't open the door for anyone you don't know," as if the minute she and Dirk the Jerk pulled off in the Jerkmobile a whole army of sneaky murderers was going to line up and start ringing the bell and saying "Pizza delivery" in fake, singsongy voices.

I nodded and nodded, and finally told Mom that they were going to be late if they didn't hurry up and leave right then, and that she should have fun and not worry about Caro and me, we'd be fine. Even then, she made a whole big deal of kissing us both and saying how her babies were all grown up, which ended up scaring Carolyn so bad she started to cry, because with all the fanfare, she got it in her head that maybe her parents were leaving for a month, or all eternity. So we had to calm her down and reassure her, and by the time that had been accomplished, Dirk the Jerk was in a foul mood and barking at Mom because they actually were late now, and his master plan to get tanked on free cocktails before the meal was in serious jeopardy.

"Way to ruin the date before it even starts, you butt hat," I said under my breath as I watched them walk to the car, bickering loud enough that I could hear them through the closed window, my mom looking precarious and uncomfortable in her high heels. And of course Carolyn heard me, so for the next forty-five minutes, while we ate the frozen lasagna Mom had left us ("Don't forget to turn the oven off when it's done, Ike!"), she insisted on calling everybody and everything a butt hat, including each bite of lasagna either one of us took and all her stuffed animals. I knew better than to draw attention to the term by telling her to stop, so I just sat there and waited for her to move on to something else. In theory, it seems like it might be funny to hear a little kid curse, but really it's kind of gross and sad.

My plan for the evening was: Get Carolyn in bed as soon as possible, then call Claire and see if she could snag a ride over so we could study for an Earth Science test. An Earth Science test called Getting to First Base.

The first part was easy. Carolyn finally understands what deals are, and she loves making them. Dirk the Jerk actually attempted to introduce her to the concept of the deal when she was about two, which is way too early for a kid to wrap her mind around something like give-and-take, but then what Dirk the Jerk doesn't know about kids could fill a warehouse. For years, he'd be like, "Okay, Carolyn, here's the deal: If you eat all your peas, I'll read you one story," and she'd be like, "No, *here's* the deal. I eat *none* of my peas, and you read me a *million* stories," and he'd get all frustrated and stalk off and make my mom take over.

Anyway, I told Caro she could have an extra Popsicle if she went to bed right away, plus I'd read her any three stories she wanted tomorrow. We shook on it, Carolyn very solemnly looking me right in the eyes the way Dirk the Jerk taught her to do when shaking hands, except she likes to do it with her eyes about five inches from yours. I got her teeth brushed, pajamaed her up, and read a chapter of *Winnie-the-Pooh*. Nightlight on, good-night kiss, outta there in fifteen minutes flat. Easy, breezy, lemon squeezy, as Carolyn likes to say. She's a way better kid that I ever was, which proves genetics isn't everything, since for all his faults my dad is still a one million percent better guy than Dirk the Jerk.

I sat down in the den and looked at the clock on the DVD player. It was seven thirty-three, and this was definitely a long shot, in that I'd only realized Babysitting = Alone at Home = Opportunity for Love this afternoon, and I hadn't wanted to call while Mom and Dirk the Jerk were around, or Carolyn, either—on top of which, the Wanzandaes shut off all electronic devices from six to seven P.M. while they ate dinner, because they were the type of family that made a big deal out of Spending Time Together. So the chances of Claire successfully springing a study session on her parents now were probably like 31 percent, but a man had to try.

HUGE pain in my ▓▓▓▓!

The normal move would have been to send her a text, but since Mom and Dirk the Jerk won't let me have a cell phone, I had to call Claire Wanzandae instead, like some kind of decrepit senior citizen. At least she has her own, so I didn't have to worry about Old Man Wanzandae picking up and grilling me about my intentions with his daughter or some old-timey junk like that—which is basically what anybody calling me has to deal with, since Dirk the Jerk insists on answering every phone call like it's some Man-of-the-House privilege, even though nobody ever calls him, because he has no friends.

Claire picked up on the second ring and said, "Hey, hold on one sec." I heard some clinking sounds and running water and then the shoosh of fabric as Claire shoved the phone into her pocket. Then nothing, and then the shoosh again, and then the closing of what was probably Claire Wanzandae's bedroom door. Then, "Hey, what's up?"

"Oh, nothing," I said, suddenly realizing that asking her to come over to my empty house was kind of a transparent move, and maybe girls didn't like that, since half of dating on a junior high school level seems to be constructing fake-accidental scenarios, as if you need to be able to deny that you ever intended to be in the same place at the same time. Like you were heisting jewels or something.

But then I decided no, why play games? Claire Wanzandae and I were beyond that now. We'd kissed three times, once in my driveway and twice in school, and even though the two in school were both super quick—me basically dawdling until the bell rang and the hallway emptied, and Claire looking both ways first like she was crossing the street, or she was a Montague and I was a Capulet, and then pecking me on the mouth—they still definitely counted.

"I was wondering if you wanted to come over," I said, cool as a polar bear's toenails. "I'm babysitting, but my sister is asleep. We could, like, watch a movie or whatever."

There was a little moment of silence on Claire's end, just enough for my stomach to fall out of my butt with fear that I'd said something wrong.

"There's no way my parents will let me go out on a school night," she said slowly, almost like she pitied me for (a) being so dumb I thought they might or (b) having such negligent parents myself. "Maybe if we had a test to study for or something," she went on, and I was about to suggest that she could tell them we did when Claire's voice dropped down to an almost-whisper and she said, "A bunch of us are sneaking out tonight. We're meeting at one A.M. at the playground in back of Cabot Elementary. Can you get out?"

Now it was my turn to be silent. I knew from Ryan Demphill that sneaking out in the middle of the night was a thing now, but I didn't know it was a thing Claire did—though maybe this was her first time. According to Ryan, you basically just goofed around on the playground, and maybe drank some Jungle Juice if somebody brought some, or lit some Roman candles, or you rode bikes through the quiet streets. It had sounded halfway dumb and halfway thrilling when he'd told me about it.

None of that sounded like Claire, though. And who was this Us, this Bunch of Us? It certainly wasn't the Us of me and Claire, which was the main Us I wanted her to focus on.

My ear felt sweaty against the phone, and I spoke without really thinking.

"How come you didn't invite me?"

"What do you mean?" Claire said. "I'm inviting you now."

"Yeah, but only because I called you," I pointed out, my voice sounding weirdly high and strangled. *Is this our first fight?* I wondered. *And if so, is it my fault?* I thought about Mom and Dirk the Jerk, snapping at each other in the driveway as they left for what was probably their only real date of the month, and wondered if that was what the future held for me and Claire.

"Don't be mad," she said, which for some reason had the effect of making me mad, probably because I'm an idiot. "It's just some kids from my elementary school. I didn't think to invite you, because you live like six miles away. But you should totally come. If you can."

That all made perfect sense. The beach ball of anger inside me deflated, and an equally large beach ball of frustration started blowing itself up instead. "I probably can't, unless my parents get home early. I can't leave Carolyn alone."

"It'll probably be stupid anyway," Claire said quickly. "I'm just going because, you know, whatever."

"Uh-huh," I said, but my mind was racing for a way to make it work. I didn't like the idea of Claire hanging out at her old elementary school at one in the morning with a bunch of kids drinking Jungle Juice—including Mark Giroux, probably, who'd also gone to Cabot. This was how you turned into Any Guy: by not being there when adventure and lacrosse players were around.

Maybe I could convince Carolyn to pretend she was sick, call Mom on her cell phone, and tell her to come home.

HUGE pain in my ▓▓▓▓!

That was stupid for about a thousand reasons.

Maybe I could call her and say that there had been an intruder—that somebody had tried to get into the house. She'd definitely come home if I said that.

She'd also probably call the police, and I'd have to lie to them, too, and if I messed up the story or they dusted for fingerprints or DNA or whatever and figured out that I was lying, they'd probably take me to jail. Plus, if I said *intruder*, who knew what Dirk the Jerk would do. Maybe decide to play Alpha Male and sit up all night with a baseball bat, defending the Ol' Homestead. So that was also dumb.

Maybe I could call Ryan and ask him to sneak out of his house and come stay with Carolyn while I met Claire. He could sleep in my bed until I got back, and nobody would be the wiser.

That wasn't so bad, actually. It wouldn't ruin Mom's night, and as an added bonus, it would show Ryan that he wasn't the only one who could get girls to like him and do cool rebel stuff.

Also, I had no other ideas.

I told Claire I'd call her back, hung up, and dialed Ryan.

"You know you're the only person who still calls me?" was the way he answered the phone.

"Why?" I said, thinking, *Easy come, easy go, Mr. Popular.* "What happened?"

"No, dummy, I mean everybody else just texts. What's up?"

"Nothing," I said. "What's up with you?" Which you have to say, even if it isn't true. Space aliens could be implanting an egg sac in your brain, and you'd still have to say "Nothing, what's up with you" before you went into it.

"Nothing."

I heard a *thump-thrack,* which meant that Ryan was lying on his bed, throwing one of his dad's racquetballs against the wall and catching it, a thing he'd been doing practically nonstop since the third grade.

"So, hey," I said. "I need a favor. Claire and a bunch of Cabot kids are sneaking out tonight, and she invited me to come."

The *thump-thrack* stopped. "All *right,* dude. Now you're talking. What time?"

"One," I said. "But listen, man—"

"How far you get with her so far?" he interrupted. "You French her yet?"

"Not yet," I said, "but listen. I'm babysitting Carolyn. Can you come over here and, like, pretend to be me so I can go?"

HUGE pain in my ▓▓▓▓!

"Uh, I think your mom can probably tell us apart, dude," Ryan said.

"No, I mean just go to sleep in my bed. The most she'll do is open the door and look in on you."

"Let me get this straight. You want me to risk getting grounded for all eternity so you can go sneaking around with some girl?"

I paused for a second, trying to gauge whether he was really mad or just playing it up, then said, "Yeah, basically."

"I'd be honored," Ryan said. "It's about time you stepped up, Saturday." And for the first time in a while, it felt like we were really friends again, not Master and Apprentice or Don Juan and Dipstick.

"Thanks," I said. "What time can you get out?"

"Like midnight," Ryan said, very matter-of-fact, and the *thump-thrack* started up again. "What time are your mom and The Jerk coming home?"

"The party ends at one, so probably like one forty-five, two."

*Thump-thrack.* "Bring a six-pack with you tonight. You'll be a hero. Trust me." And Ryan hung up.

I went down to the basement and took a look at the cases of beer Dirk the Jerk had piled up in the refrigerator there. He bought it in bulk at Costco about once a month, and he got whatever was on sale. You'd think a boozehound like Dirk the Jerk would be particular about his brand, but I guess he was more concerned with saving a few bucks.

He had two six-packs of Amstel Light left, and then three unopened cases of Miller Genuine Draft, and one sixer of McMurtrie's Driving Through the Snow Yuletide Xmas Ale, with a picture of Santa driving a sleigh on the cardboard holder. I grabbed that, figuring it was only April and he wouldn't miss it for a while. Plus, I figured that if McMurtrie was making beer specifically for Christmas, that probably meant he was some kind of Master Brewer or whatever.

I stashed it in my backpack, went upstairs, and checked the clock. It was seven fifty-nine. I decided to take a nap, tomorrow being a school day and all, but right away I knew I was too excited. In fact, I felt super alert—like a criminal mastermind, my brain calculating every angle of the caper.

Angle #1 was: strolling back in through the front door was too risky. If I made any noise and somebody came downstairs, I'd be caught red-handed.

That's when inspiration struck. I hustled back down to the basement and opened one of the storm windows that leads to the front yard at ground level. Then I double-timed both flights of stairs up to my room, grabbed a set of pajamas, came back to the basement, and stashed them under a pile of random junk. Now if Mom or Dirk the Jerk somehow heard me come back in, I'd be wearing pajamas and there'd be nothing for them to be suspicious about. I could say I hadn't been able to sleep and I'd gone to look through one of the old photo albums that are stashed down there, and they'd assume I was missing my dad and basically leave me alone, since neither one of them really knows what to say about that.

It was going to be the perfect crime.

# CHAPTER 12

It wasn't the perfect crime.

In fact, when I look back years from now—from my eight-by-ten prison cell, or my nice, comfy refrigerator carton underneath the highway overpass, or my tour bus where I'm traveling as a roadie for Justin Bieber—I'll probably pinpoint that night as the moment my life turned into a poop soufflé.

When I left my house at twelve eleven, I was on top of the world, biking through the silent streets with a heart full of excitement and a backpack full of beer. I felt vigorous and strong and confident, like I was facing the world head-on, plunging into the new adventure of teenage love with gusto, unafraid to break the rules if that was what it took. The night air was crisp and perfect, like an apple, or Halloween, and

HUGE pain in my ▓▓▓▓!

I was flying toward my destiny. I'd showered right before I left, and slapped on some of Dirk the Jerk's aftershave, because the new Ike Saturday thinks of Everything.

Even Ryan had been impressed. "You're totally getting to first base," he told me right before I left, and extended his fist for me to bump. I didn't really like the way he said it, but I bumped him anyway. The rest of his advice had been pretty smart: to remember that all the rest of these kids had gone to school together since kindergarten, seen each other cry and strike out playing kickball and blow out birthday candles and all that stuff. I, on the other hand, was a mysterious outsider. I could be anybody I had the courage to conjure up.

I liked the sound of that. I mulled it over as I biked, and it made me think of my dad. Maybe he'd gotten out to California and decided he could also be anybody he wanted. Maybe he had a girlfriend who made him feel good about himself, though if he did, he'd never mentioned her to me.

Then I thought about my mom and whether she'd decided to be anybody she wanted after the divorce. She had gotten these blond streaks called highlights in her hair, and for a while she'd done a ton of yoga—a couple of times I'd even gone with her, to this kids-and-parents class that was sort of fun. Maybe she'd thought yoga class would be a good place to meet a guy, since one of her main complaints about my dad was that he wasn't open-minded enough and never wanted to do new stuff like yoga or ballroom dancing with her. But instead she'd met The Jerk at a Christmas party. As far as I could tell, he was no more into yoga or ballroom dancing than my dad was, but I never heard her talk about wanting to do that stuff now anyway.

I was the first to arrive at Cabot Elementary even though I lived about fifteen times farther away than any of them. I would have preferred to show up late, but then I figured, *Nope, don't think like that, invent yourself into coolness, make it work.* I looked around the playground—which was a typical elementary school setup, with a jungle gym and tire swings and regular swings, straight metal slide and plastic twisty slide—as if it were a movie set and decided where and how I wanted to be when Claire and the rest showed up. The answer was: chilling on a swing, taking casual swigs from a beer. Like a straight-up gangster.

The only problem was, I hadn't thought to bring a bottle opener. I tried positioning the serrated rim of the bottle cap against the wood edge of the jungle gym and chopping down with the heel of my hand, but no dice. I felt a drop of sweat roll down the inside of my arm—not from the exertion, but from picturing the lameness of Claire and the rest rolling up to find me sitting there with an unopened beer in my lap. So I walked over to the brick wall of the school, figuring that if I angled the bottle right, I could kind of scrape the cap off, like against a little ridge of mortar or whatever.

That didn't work, either. Any minute now, they were going to show up and find me acting like a moron, and I couldn't have that. I looked around the playground, trying to think like an inventor, or a wilderness expert, and then the thought *What would Ben Franklin do?* flashed across my mind.

I circled back to the big play structure, and—boom—inspiration struck. I walked underneath the tallest part, wedged the top of the bottle up between two of the thick wood slats, and jerked sideways. Success. The bottle cap fell to the ground by my feet, and I took a nice long celebratory pull of McMurtie's Driving Through the Snow Yuletide Xmas Brew.

I basically hate the taste of beer, but just then it was exactly like it's supposed to be in beer ads, as cool and refreshing as a snowcapped mountain you can drink. I gulped down a good half of the bottle all at once, feeling myself gliding into the role of Bad Boy From the Other Side of Town as the bubbles slid down my throat, then popped the bottle off my lips like a cowboy and swiped the back of my hand across my mouth.

It came away streaked with blood. I took a closer look at the bottle and saw that I'd (a) chipped the glass when I'd opened it, and (b) stabbed myself in the lower lip when I took that big tough-guy chugalug.

A fat crimson drop splatted onto my forearm, and then another. I don't know if you've ever cut your lip, but approximately half the blood in your body turns out to be concentrated there. Another splat, onto my shirt this time. I lifted the hem to my face, tried to apply pressure and staunch the bleeding while my brain alternated between chanting, *Please don't let them show up now* and *How am I going to make out with Claire Wanzandae like this?*

The bleeding stopped after a little while, possibly because I had no more blood left in my lip. My shirt was spattered with red drops, and who knew what my face looked like? I had to get cleaned up, and fast—in my mind, I could already hear Mark Giroux saying, *Uh, you know you're covered in blood, bro?* I ran to the water fountain, but it was broken.

I was feeling light-headed, maybe from the loss of blood but probably from downing half a beer in three seconds, and my thinking was a little muddled. For a few seconds I just stood there, staring at the broken fountain the way a dog that's about to puke stares at the ground. Then I poured some beer into my palm, and washed my face with it. I tried to use the spigot of the water fountain as a mirror, but it wasn't shiny, and the moonlight was too pale anyway. My face felt sticky, and my lip was throbbing. My hand felt sticky, too. There was about a third of the beer left, and I drank it down without hurting myself any more.

Then I realized I wouldn't be holding a beer when they arrived, so I opened another one, using the same method as before but being way more careful and precise. The cap popped off, *no problemo*, and I carried the bottle over to my swing and sat down, feeling a lot less cool and wondering if I was drunk or buzzed or what. I knew I shouldn't drink this second beer, but then I started imagining Mark Giroux noticing that it was full and saying stuff like *Dude, it only works if you drink it*. I swallowed two or three mouthfuls, just so it wouldn't look weird.

I must have sat there for another fifteen minutes before anybody showed up, and I guess I drank most of the second beer. If you're alone with nothing to do and a beer in your hand, it's kind of hard not to drink. It's also not the easiest thing in the world to figure out whether you've had too much.

It gets easier to determine when Claire Wanzandae, Mark Giroux, Pascale Berry, Rob Tannenbaum, and Eric Lasner arrive on their bikes and you call out "Yo," and the single word feels like a huge marble, rolling around in your mouth.

I stood up, forgetting all about the little Diorama of Coolness I'd been constructing. Claire was skipping toward me, her hair flying out behind her. Playgrounds make everybody want to act like a little kid, I guess. A little kid or a drunk.

"You made it!" she said, and gave me a quick hug, cheek-to-cheek.

"Yup." I kind of burbled the word, a little off balance from the hug action.

Claire scrunched up her nose. "You smell like beer." She didn't sound excited about it.

"Oh yeah," I said as the other kids all shambled over from their bikes. "I brought beer." I jogged over to the jungle gym, feeling like the ground was made of pudding, and pulled the rest of the six-pack out of my backpack. It had been a thing of majesty when I swiped it from Dirk the Jerk, but now it looked kind of forlorn, with the two bottles missing.

Mark Giroux didn't think so, though. "Saturday, nice!" he said, sliding a bottle out of the cardboard holder and popping the cap with the opener attached to his keychain in, like, point-three nanoseconds. Seriously—a bottle opener on his keychain. What do Mark Giroux's parents think that's for? Camping emergencies? Sodas from the 1950s?

Rob and Eric were already lunging for brews, too, but just in time I remembered something else Ryan had taught me in the first couple weeks of school, when he'd just become King Stud and wanted nothing more than to share all his new wisdom about girls. Which was: a slick move is to make other guys look like uncivilized goons, if you can do it in a super low-key way. Like, if they're all scrounging to get one of the remaining three beers, you pull some Chivalry and offer them to the girls instead, and the other guys have to be like "Uh, oh yeah, duh."

"Whoa, whoa, whoa," I said, swinging the sixer away from them like my arm was a pendulum. "Ladies, can I offer you a beverage?"

Pascale said, "Thank you, Ike," with a large amount of ceremoniousness, and then added, "I'm glad someone is a gentleman."

Touchdown.

She took a bottle and passed it to Mark, to open for her.
"Claire?" I said.

"I don't drink," Claire said, a little coldly. Or maybe it was my imagination.

"You want the last one, dude?" Rob asked me.

"Go ahead," I told him. "I already had two."

"Whoa, Saturday," said Mark, and extended his fist the same way Ryan had, for some bro-to-bro fist-bump action.

I could definitely feel a kind of chilliness coming off Claire now, but I decided to ignore it. I mean, Mark Giroux was showing me respect. Pascale Berry, who is also extremely cute, was calling me a gentleman, and everybody was drinking my beer. I felt loose and good, as if the beer had negotiated a treaty with my body and everybody was a winner.

Meanwhile, Rob Tannenbaum was rummaging around in his own backpack. "I brought something, too," he said, and I expected him to pull out some booze, but instead he revealed a bag of kettle corn.

I expected the reaction to be kind of disappointed, but Mark Giroux said, "Nice," and dug his hand into the bag.

*Aha*, I thought. This was an opportunity to cement my fake reputation as the Bad Boy From the Other Side of Town Who Is Kind of a Jerk.

"Yeah, if you're a five-year-old," I said. "Did you bring some blocks for us to play with, too?"

"I love kettle corn," said Pascale Berry, digging in.

I turned toward her, and with the beer fizzing up into my brain, I felt kind of weightless and dizzy, and also the words coming out of my mouth started to feel like they were a long way away, as if my vocal cords were operating without the usual system of checks and balances and oversight committees. Like my brain was entering Government Shutdown.

"And I love drinking," I declared, lifting my beer. "You should drink, Claire. Drinking is awesome."

"It's not so awesome when your stepfather does it," Claire said, crossing her arms over her chest.

"Screw him," I said, and turned to the rest of them. "He's a jerk," I explained, and lunged for the kettle corn I'd just been making fun of.

I stuffed some in my mouth, and then said, "You know who else likes to drink?" Possibly way too loud.

"Who?" said Mark Giroux.

"Ben Franklin," I announced.

"Wow, dude," said Mark. "You're for-real obsessed with Ben Franklin, huh?" He took a sip of beer and jerked his thumb at me. "We had to write letters to famous people for

History class. This dude wrote to Franklin, and, like, wouldn't let anybody read it. What's with you and Ben Franklin, dude?"

"Nothing," I said, feeling more blurry with each second that passed. "He liked to party, is all."

"All those dudes did," Eric declared. "They were, like, 'Oh, hey, freakin'…let's do some shots before we write the… Gettysburg Address or whatever.'" Eric is not in Honors History.

"Exactly," I said, for no reason whatsoever except a sudden feeling of camaraderie with Eric, who had never even spoken to me before. I spun toward Claire. "Right, Claire? Claire likes Ben Franklin, too. We actually…" And then I broke off, because even through the haze of drunkenness, which was getting thicker by the second, I could see that the look on her face was *Shut Up, Ike*.

"You actually what?" Pascale wanted to know.

"Nothing," I said. "Forget it. Hey, Claire, do you, uh… should we go on the swings?"

The moment I said it, I wanted to punch myself in the neck. I might as well have said, "Hey, Claire, how about I make an excuse so we can leave and I can try to kiss you?"

Everybody waited to see what she'd say. Meanwhile, the beer and lasagna and kettle corn were circling one another warily inside my gut, like three strange dogs meeting on the street, sniffing one another's hind parts and trying to decide whether to fight or frolic or ignore.

Finally, Claire Wanzandae said, "Okay," and started walking back in that direction.

"See you lovebirds later," Mark Giroux said as I followed Claire around the side of the jungle gym, just soft enough that I caught it but she didn't, a real Cool Bro move.

She was already sitting on a swing when I rounded the bend, her knees bowed together and the toes of her Converse All-Stars just barely grazing the ground. I plopped down on the other one, grabbed the chains, and made a quarter-twist, so I was facing her. Claire just kept on swaying ever-so-slightly back and forth.

"Hey," I said. "You mad at me or something?"

She glanced at me, then did a double take and scowled and turned her whole body in my direction.

"You're bleeding," Claire said, and tapped a finger to her lip. I mirrored her, and when I brought my hand away, sure enough, there was a smeared wet bead of red.

"Oh yeah," I said, the words sounding slushy in my ears. "I broke a beer bottle earlier, trying to open it, and cut my lip. But hey, it's no big deal, what can…"

Claire turned away, and I stopped talking.

"You're different when you drink," she said, kind of bitterly, like we'd had this conversation a hundred times before or something.

*This is the first time I ever drank* is what I thought, but instead for some reason I said, "Come on, Claire, give it a rest." Which is a total Dirk-the-Jerk-to-Mom line, and why it was coming out of my mouth, I couldn't imagine and didn't really want to think about.

Claire Wanzandae stood up like something had stung her on the butt, rested her hands on her hips, and flashed her eyes, and said, "Ex*cuse* me?"

It was like she'd pulled the rip cord on my reality parachute, and all at once I realized what a fool and a jerk I'd been tonight, and my whole soul filled up with, like, this sorrowful desire to make it right, to let Claire know I was only doing all these stupid drunken things because I wanted to impress her, that she was right and I was sorry and to please just give me a hug and tell me everything wasn't ruined and trashed forever.

I rose. "Claire," I said, moving in close and taking her hand. "Listen—"

At that exact moment, the beer and lasagna and kettle

corn inside me decided they didn't like each other after all—that, actually, they were mortal enemies. My stomach curled up like a piece of paper catching fire, and with zero percent warning I vomited all over my one true love, my ex–future wife, my lab partner and soul mate, the beautiful and brilliant Claire Sasha Wanzandae.

To say that it was the worst moment of my life is an understatement. In many ways, it was the last moment of my life, or at least the end of everything good or promising or not super crappy. Even in the best-case puking-on-your-crush scenario, it's a very hard thing for a relationship to recover from. But this was not that scenario. Not not not.

Not.

Number one is, Claire hates throw-up. Obviously everybody hates throw-up, and being thrown up on, but for Claire it's a *phobia*. She can't even watch somebody puke in a movie. She can barely say the word.

So, she screamed at the top of her lungs. Not once, not twice. Actually, maybe it was once, but that once lasted about two minutes. And in that two minutes, the lights came on in all the houses across the street from Cabot Elementary, and somebody, or everybody, called 9-1-1 to report that a very slow, painful, and incompetent murder was being committed on the local playground.

I guess you could say that Claire was in shock. There wasn't much I could do to calm her down, because this particular type of puking was not a one-and-done type of experience. It took time. It came in waves. I don't really want to say any more about this, actually, because I'm starting to feel sick all over again just thinking about it.

The smart thing to do would have been to get the heck away from there, as fast as possible. But I was too sick, and Claire was too out of her mind. The rest of the crew divided the next ninety seconds between trying to chill her out (Eric, Rob, Mark) and tending to Puking Ike (Pascale).

Then something happened that made the Evening So Far feel like a trip to Six Flags Discovery Kingdom.

Mark Giroux looked at the label of his beer bottle and starting laughing. He nudged Rob and Eric, and suddenly all three of them were doubled over in hysterics.

"Hey, dude," Mark said finally, to me. "Have you had anything else to drink tonight?"

I shook my head. "Just those beers," I said.

"Wow," he said, actually sweating from laughter. "That's kind of amazing, Saturday. Because this is nonalcoholic

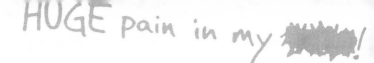
HUGE pain in my ▓▓▓▓!

beer." He held it up. "See? 'Driving Through the Snow.'
Like, don't drive drunk."

Suddenly, I felt very, very sober.

That was when the cops showed up.

# CHAPTER 13

Usually, even if your life has turned into one big, melty poopsicle, there is some part of it that is still okay. And you've just got to focus on that part and get all the enjoyment you can from it and wait for the bad parts to get better. Like, when things between my parents started getting really bad—in the sense that any time the two of them were in a room together they would start off smiling and trying to be nice but you could tell it was a strain, and pretty soon they'd be yelling at each other, and also yelling "not in front of Ike," and even though I couldn't figure out what the problem was, I knew it was awful to live like that, which was why when they sat me down to tell me they still loved me and it wasn't my fault but sometimes people shouldn't live together, blah blah blah, I basically wanted to high-five them both for finally coming to their senses—when all that was happening, at least there was school. School was super fun that year, because it basically wasn't school yet, it was just first grade, which is like ten minutes of adding up three carrots plus two carrots equals five carrots, ten minutes of learning that the letter *A* makes an *A* sound, and then six hours of playing soccer and eating snacks and listening to stories. That was also the year Ryan Demphill and I got super close, because we were desk-mates and that bonds you with a guy for life, like going to war together.

Or when Dirk the Jerk moved in, not that long afterward, there was Carolyn, who is pretty much the most rad person I've ever met.

But now there was nothing. I mean, there was still Carolyn, but some problems you can't ask a five-year-old to solve. And even Carolyn was treating me kind of weird, because she sensed that I must have done something really, really bad for Mom to treat me so cold.

When the cops brought me home, Mom and Dirk the Jerk had just gotten home from their party like two minutes before. I was feeling better by then—or, at least, the horrible feeling in my stomach was not about lasagna or beer or kettle corn anymore. It was about fear and shame. Which, let me tell you, can also make a guy feel like puking, even if a guy has already puked all the puke he can puke.

Mom opened the door and took one look at me and the lady cop who'd walked me to the door, and her eyes got wide with terror, and she grabbed me in her arms on instinct and said, "What happened? Where's your sister?"

"She's upstairs," I said, and I felt a little bit of slackness come into her hug and knew that in about three seconds she was going to stop being relieved that everybody was safe and start being furious and extremely inquisitive. And also that in about seven seconds, Dirk the Jerk was going to wander in and add a big dose of Jerkiness to the situation.

"Ma'am, your son and his friends were drinking beer on the playground of Cabot Elementary School," the cop said in a super-stern but super-bored voice, like this was all one big distraction from the high-speed car chase she was supposed to be having right now.

"Not real beer," I said into my mother's shoulder. "Nonalcoholic beer." I thought about adding *Not real friends, either*, but I didn't.

In a flash, my mother pulled away and squeezed my upper arms with her hands, as tight as those cuffs they put on you when they take your blood pressure. And she kind of shook me. And said, "You left your sister here *alone?*"

For a second, I couldn't speak. I'd never seen her this angry. I halfway expected her to tell the cop she wanted to press charges against me or something.

"No," I said finally. "Of course not. Ryan is here."

Her eyes got narrow, and she exhaled hard, like a tired horse. Then she crinkled up her nose, probably getting a whiff of the vomit/beer scent coming off me. Which was strong.

"Go take a shower and go to sleep," she said, in a voice like a bullwhip. "And tell Ryan to go home. I'll deal with you tomorrow."

I barely remember falling asleep, but when I woke up it was almost noon. Which seemed like a good thing at the time, not having to go to school—a chance for everything to blow over, and maybe evidence that my mom was going to show me some mercy. My whole body felt sore. Throwing up uses muscles you did not even know you had.

I walked downstairs and found Mom sitting at the kitchen table, waiting for me. I went to the cabinet and took out some cereal, but she said, "Sit down, Ike," before I could pour it. I was super hungry, but I did what I was told.

I was expecting some yelling, but instead she just stared at me for what seemed like forever, with this look of sad befuddlement, like she had no idea who I was or how I'd become such a monster.

Getting looked at like that was really awful. "I'm sorry," I said. "I'm probably grounded for, like, a month, right?" Which sometimes works, to kind of slickly suggest a punishment you can handle, but make it sound like, *Oh no, anything but that.*

"Much longer," Mom said. "But that's not important, Ike. What's important is trust. I've always been able to trust you. And now I can't. You're going to have to prove to me that you can be trusted again." A tear fell out of her eye and rolled down her cheek, and I felt like digging a hole and crawling inside it and curling up into a little wretched ball.

"How?" I said, in a gravelly little whisper. If she had said *By eating this live snake,* I would have done it, no questions asked.

But all she said was, "I don't know," and a big sob jumped out of her throat, and I felt like digging a hole inside the hole, and crawling into that.

\* \* \*

I didn't get the day off after all. I ate my bowl of cereal, basically gulping the flakes down past the lump of sadness in my throat, and then my mom drove me to school. I got there a couple of minutes after Earth Science started, and managed to slip in the door without Mrs. Broussard noticing that I was late.

Claire was already sorting a bunch of rock samples in a tray at our workstation.

"Hi," I said, giving her a smile of, like, *Mistakes were made, but hey, here we are, no harm no foul.*

She half turned away from me and didn't answer. I started to get a bad feeling in my still-not-right gut, but I ignored it and kept talking.

"What did your parents do?" I asked. "Mine flipped out. I'm grounded indefinitely. What a night, huh?"

I sort of knew she wasn't going to say anything, even before she didn't say anything. But for some reason, such as being a moron, I had it in my head that if I just kept acting like everything was normal and she wasn't mad at me, then it would end up being that way. So I said, "I'm pretty sure it was food poisoning that made me so sick. I mean, obviously it wasn't—"

Claire Wanzandae spun toward me on her heel, and her beautiful hair spun with her, but a second later. "Let's just do the experiment," she said, and her mouth looked hard, like she was in the early stages of turning into a very cute but angry statue.

"Okay," I said. "I just—"

She spun back away from me, and for the rest of the period the only words she said were *igneous, sedimentary,* and *metamorphic.* And when the bell rang, she grabbed her bag and speed-walked out of the room like it was full of poison gas.

I gathered my stuff up slowly, feeling like I wanted to burst into tears, and walked into the hallway, which was full of kids shouting and goofing around and getting things from their lockers, just like it always is between classes. But it all seemed very distant and far away now, as if I were observing the strange rituals of a newly discovered tribe in some remote part of the world.

That didn't last long, because the members of this tribe knew all about me.

"Way to get everybody busted, Saturday," called a kid named Evan from my gym class as he passed by.

"Hey, Ike," said a girl whose name I didn't even know, an eighth grader on the soccer team. I looked over at her, and she thrust a bottle of Snapple at me. "Want a sip of my iced tea, or will it make you drunk?" And everybody within earshot started laughing.

This was very, very bad.

I ignored her and kept walking. But there was nowhere to go. I was the worst kind of famous, and I might as well have been walking around Thomas J. Harden Junior High wearing a shirt made out of dog turds, for all anybody wanted to do with me.

# CHAPTER 14

My Dear Franklin—

If the possessive *my* in this salutation—a declaration of affection traditionally reserved for one's betrothed or, in its least, directed to a person whom the letter writer beholds with a fondness far exceeding the temperate nature of a casual correspondence—surprises you, I believe the reason will render itself evident a few paragraphs hence.

I choose first, however, to register my utter bewilderment in regard to your indictments of my fellow Committee members for acts committed at times that have yet to occur. A war in 1812? A death in 1800? Thomas Jefferson's tryst with someone named

Dolley Madison? And though I am hesitant to offer correction, a profound appreciation for irony compels me to indicate that you are in error in your spelling of gaggle, as opposed to your *Google*, an occurrence this Founding Father finds most incongruous given how you chided me, in your initial missive, for capitalizing letters Unnecessarily.

Yet I find myself intrigued by your offer to provide me with information about events that have not happened, as I would like nothing more than to, may Providence forgive me for what I am about to repeat, "Screw over Jefferson and the rest of those clowns." Because on the off chance that you are not wrong-headed in your insistence that you take residence in a time in my distant future, there is one question to which an answer would be most appreciated.

In particular, will the symbol of our new nation, should we succeed in our campaign for independence—the emblem that would appear on our currency, engraved in stone above our pillared doorways, and sitting atop our new flagpoles—be the bald eagle or, as I most ardently contend for, the wild turkey?

At this moment, I am in spirited debate with my most estimable colleagues, whom I truly believe are in errata in their contention that it should be the former. The bald eagle is a Bird of bad moral character, as he does not come by his living honestly. No doubt you have seen him perched on some dead tree near the River, where, too lazy to fish for himself, he watches the labour of the Fishing Hawk and when that diligent bird has at length taken a Fish and is carrying it back to the awaiting mouths of his young ones, that dastardly eagle swoops down and takes it from him.

Whereas the turkey, by comparison, is a nobler Bird and an original Native of America—one that greeted the Separatists upon their arrival at Plymouth Rock and was thus rewarded with a place of Honour at their Feast of thanksgiving. Though vain and a bit silly, the turkey is most notably a bird of courage that would not hesitate to attack a Grenadier of the British arms who would invade his farmyard with a red Coat on.

Though I continue to regard you as either foolhardy

or the victim of a head wound, in your insistence as to the year you write from, my perspectives as both a scientist and philosopher have often allowed for a degree of credence as to the possibilities of time travel, and it is thus that I offer a benefit of doubt. Therefore, my request of you, dear Franklin, is to inform me if I will have Held sway and provide me with proof of the outcome of this contention. Should there be a note of legal tender with a wild turkey on it, do send along a single bill. (Fret not, for I shall promptly repay in kind.) Or should a troop of uniformed lads who have reached the highest rank in a boys' youth organization and are admiringly referred to as Turkey Scouts march in formation down a main street during a parade, I encourage your posting an Edition of a periodical bearing the date in which you claim to exist. Enclosed herewith, please find what I believe to be more than sufficient postage.

And now to the matter of Claire Wanzandae and your stated dissonance in regard to how "any guy" can sustain a relationship with such an exalted object of desire. For this I request your indulgence, whilst I allude to a parallel episode that, furthermore, serves to justify the "My Dear" at the outset of this letter.

After the death of Deborah, my beloved wife of forty-four years, I was bereaved beyond description. And though much has been made of my romantic endeavors in these ensuing years, there are the affections of one particular woman that I seek to obtain. This would be Madame Helvetius, a most comely widow. Though she is unable to fill the void left by my departed Deborah's appointment with our Lord, this lady provides such haven that I wish to extend a proposal of marriage. Yet, despite my multitudinous accomplishments, I have been timid and in lack of the Confidence to approach her because of my "stringy hair." Therefore, I was intrigued by your mention of a formula with the ability to provide luster and body to what, to my grave misfortune, has born resemblance to the incorrigible strands on a coconut since I was eleven years Of age. And though no such conditioner exists here in 1776 Philadelphia (I state this with an absence of equivocation after I sought the hair salon.com you cited with disappointing results), I was so inspired by your words that I summoned my acumen as a man of science and employed the meaty leaves from a succulent plant commonly referred to as Aloe Vera in concocting my own follicle-enhancing poultice. And it is with boundless merriment and jaunted step that I unveil, after but a dozen applications, the visage I shall present to Madame Helvetius on the occasion of my request for her hand, whensoever as my business in Committee comes to an end and I have occasion to make a triumphant return to France.

And it is for this that I offer most heartfelt gratitude, my Dear Franklin.

I remain,
Benjamin Franklin

# CHAPTER 15

April 29, 2014

Dear B to the F-R,

Okay, first of all, my mind is blown right now for a Number of reasons. But let me start by saying, your latest Missive is the first communication I have had with the Outside World in Several days. Due to circumstances too Painful to go into fully, I have been grounded in Perpetuity by my mom and Dirk the Jerk, as a result of being brought home at two in the morning by an officer of the Law when I was supposed to be home babysitting my sister but had instead conspired to have Ryan Demphill pretend to be me so I could meet Claire Wanzandae for some Merriment or whatever.

# HUGE pain in my ▓▓▓!

Since then, Claire has not spoken to me except as Necessary, which is worse than not At all. I understand that I acted like a toolbox, Ben Franklin, and also that I expelled the Contents of my stomach on her as a result of thinking I was Drunk as a Diplomat, though actually that was all in my Mind as the beer I imbibed contained no alcohol. I know that girls, and people in general, do not like to be vomited On, but it doesn't seem to me like a reason to ignore Forever a person you previously liked in a major and Growing way. But Claire Wanzandae does not even seem willing to let me apologize, much less give me another Chance. Much less kiss me ever again.

I don't know what to do, B-Freezy, and if you have any Wisdom to lay on me, I would appreciate it because I have no one else to turn To. A bunch of other people will not speak to me, either, because they blame me for getting them busted and grounded as well. Pretty much the whole school knows about these Disgraceful Events, so I am living the life of a Social Outcast and Walking Joke. Even Ryan Demphill is acting cold to me, partly because my mom called his mom and ratted him out for sneaking over to our house, and partly because being cold to Ike is the popular thing to Do.

But on to bigger and better stuff, Ben Franklin. I will admit that I have been skeptical about you. I didn't really believe that you were you, or that you were writing from the Past. I thought somebody was Yanking my chain in the Present, because it makes no sense according to the world as I know it that letters could travel back and forth in time. I mean, let's be honest, Ben Franklin. The very idea is completely Bonkers.

But when I opened your last envelope and found a whole Boatload of stamps from 1776 inside, I was forced to rethink my position. I can't see somebody having that Quantity of old-timey stamps on hand, and even if they did, I doubt they would give them away to some random Bozo as you did, because they are quite Valuable. Besides which, every single Thing you have written about in any of your letters Checks Out. Nobody could pretend so Well to know the things you Know and Not Know the things you claim to be ignorant Of. Besides which, why would someone Bother?

# HUGE pain in my ▓▓▓▓!

I've been pondering all this for a full week now, Benjamin Franklin. The nature of reality. The possibility of time travel. The magic of stamps. Physics (which I have not Taken, but still).

My conclusion, for what it's worth, is this: Who am I to think I know anything about anything? Just because something hasn't been done before doesn't mean it can't be. Just because people don't believe something doesn't mean it doesn't exist, and just because people do doesn't mean it does. I mean, nobody thought the Duck-Billed Platypus was real when it was discovered by scientists in the late seventeen hundreds, because mammals aren't supposed to lay eggs, or have webbed feet. But the D-Plat was totally legit, and everybody had to re-evaluate what was true and what wasn't. If history has taught us anything, Ben Franklin, it's that human beings have believed a Ton of Incredibly Stupid Stuff. And not just believed, but been ready to kill for that stuff.

I understand that as a man of Science, you are probably just as skeptical that I am writing to you from the year 2015, so let me lay it all out for you in no uncertain

# BENJAMIN FRANKLIN

Terms. First of all, there are no Turkey Scouts. You lost
that one. The Eagle is the national bird of America, but if
I were you, I wouldn't get too bent out of shape over it.
All it really means is that you can buy a mesh trucker
hat with a picture of an eagle and a flag on it from a
drugstore if you are a redneck.

I realize this fact doesn't prove anything, which is
why I am enclosing something that ought to blow your
mind. Take a careful look at it, BF. It is a hundred-dollar
bill, a Federal Reserve Note signed by Treasurer of the
United States Anna Escobedo Cabral and Secretary of
the Treasury Henry M. LastnameIcan'tread, number
HH15680033BH8, Series 2006, marked Legal
Tender for All Debts, Public and Private. Rub the
paper between your fingertips, and notice how thick
it is. Check out the intricate little designs around the
border. Lift it to the light and appreciate the sneaky
little watermarks that prove it isn't counterfeit. But
mostly, look at the giant portrait right in the middle
of the bill.

That is YOU, B-Freezy. Your hair looks good, too, even if
your lips look slightly weird, as if maybe you were holding

a little bit of water in your mouth when this portrait was painted.

If this doesn't convince you that I am writing from the future, I don't know what will. I stole it right out of Dirk the Jerk's wallet while he was in the shower, and in a few hours he will probably notice and blame me, since I am now an Untrustworthy Lying Thief in his Opinion. But by that time, this letter will be in the mail, on its way to 1776 and to you.

I know this is a lot to think about, Ben Franklin, so I will wrap it Up with just one final question for you to ponder: Since life is such a large satchel of donkey droppings for me here in 2015, how would you feel about your Dear young buddy and namesake attempting to pay you a little visit to 1776? With all my Knowledge of the future, I could be very useful to you, I bet—a super-stealthy secret weapon against Jefferson and Adams and the rest of those cocky old statesmen, plus a secret weapon for America Herself in the struggle for Freedom. Just give me the word, Ben Franklin, and I will make a couple of sandwiches, tape myself inside the largest box I can Find, punch a few breathing holes, and hope for swift passage to your estimable Time. Because, let's face it, things could not get a lot Worse for me here in mine.

Yours Hopefully Despite My Circumstances,
Franklin the Drunk
(just kidding)

# CHAPTER 16

Dear Franklin—

Under the most ordinary of circumstances, the invocation of a personally penned saying resides beyond the comfortable borders of my nature. For purpose of example, I cite how I ceased exclaiming "Early to bed, and early to rise, makes a man healthy, wealthy, and wise" some time ago. These days, I merely go to bed early, wake up early, and allow the benefits of this strict constitution to speak for themselves.

However, your most recent missive, full of such profound longings for romance gone awry, has impell'd me to recall a proverb I wrote when only a teen—after arriving in Philadelphia and spending my last shilling on a tricornered hat that, by dint of a rather hardy autumnal gust off the harbor, flew off my head and became indelibly besmirched when it came to rest upon an especially moist specimen deposited by an oblivious Clydesdale. And as I stood there mourning the loss of my just-purchased head topper, I spontaneously uttered the words: "It is better to have loved a hat and lost, than to have walked around bareheaded your whole life."

While admittedly not among my more pithy aphorisms, it does resonate at this moment as I, like you, am suffering the loss of a beloved. To wit, my intended Madame Helvetius, who recently paid a surprise visit to Philadelphia. And to whom, over a romantic dinner, I showed the legal tender you posted to me with every hope that it would serve to impress. However, upon viewing the portrait—which, as of this writing, I have yet to sit for—she recoiled, proclaiming that without the Pompadour I presently wear, my head bears a strong resemblance to a mountain she has skied down and that she does not wish to grow old in the company of such a cranium. Whereupon she took leave of the bistro where we supped, leaving me emotionally bereft in a silent scene underscored by the plodding chords of a dirge emanating from the establishment's glass harmonica, which I now regret inventing.

My reaction induced me to the brink of dyspepsia marked by Symptoms not unlike those I suspect you bore prior to, during, and after the dousing of your beloved Claire with the still-undigested contents of Your stomach on a night you should very well have been early to bed, remained there, and been wiser upon awakening.

I, however, upon return to my home, soon bore envy that you were able to expel the rancid brew from your body, whereas I found myself in My lavatory hunched on bended knees, alternatively looking downward into an awaiting toilet and appealing skyward for assistance in the expulsion of lodged projectiles without preference as to which orifice should be deemed as the designated point Of egress.

After a seemed eternity replete with a flurry of rectal outbursts near worthy of the lightning rod

I invented, along with attendant groans such as I can only imagine one would emit while attempting to defecate the Liberty Bell, it became apparent that the good Lord was attendant to other matters and that divine intervention was not soon forthcoming.

It was then that I recalled still another forgotten Maxim of my own devising: "When in doubt, whip it out." And finding myself filled with doubt, I promptly opened my medicine cabinet and whipped out an apothecary jar of castor oil, two dollops of which coursed their Respective ways to points of concern—culminating in a torrential evacuation of morsels I recognized from a celebratory dinner I attended the night Georgia became the thirteenth colony in 1733. And leaving me with the most profound conviction that if our thirteen colonies stage a revolt tantamount to the visceral rebellion I had just endured, we shall not only win our independence but also rule the world.

So, as I write this, I am a forlorn forefather. Physically frail. And at a spiritual nadir, as my self-image has fallen victim to the vagaries of the woman I prayed could fill the emptiness once occupied by my departed Deborah.

My sullied self-image was further injured by the wording of your letter. My salutation has undergone a precipitous demise from "Dear Mr. Franklin" to "Dear B to the F-R." How is it, I ask you, that a Founding Father, printer, statesman, inventor, author, politician, scientist, musician, and philosopher held in the highest of regards by colonists, as well as heads of state abroad, should be addressed as "B-Freezy"?

And while I chose to believe that degeneration in the lexicon has been extreme, and what reads as invective to me actually represents the height of respect in your era, my sensitive condition was dealt a further indignity upon hearing of the existence of the duck-billed platypus. An egg-laying mammal? The absurdity that such an abomination could exist struck me as a further injustice to the egg-laying wild turkey, a Bird who is nowhere to be found—even with the able assistance of the bifocals I invented—on either side of the legal tender that bears my most unattractive image.

Is there no good news forthcoming, Franklin? I further query as to whether the eras that shall follow the days extant are all so...upsetting. I select this word advisedly, as a man of science, because it is of far greater concern to me that your proposed visit to 1776—besides disrupting the peaceful, nightshirt-clad tranquility of my private life—may very well upset the delicacy of the space-time continuum and engender untold galactic repercussions.

This is an uncharted multidimensional theory that, despite its Euclidean roots and most recent postulation as a mathematical concept by my esteemed colleague Jean le Rond d'Alembert, has yet to advance beyond conjecture. And so, out of respect for the tenuous nature of this beguiling hypothetic, I implore you, young Franklin, do NOT post yourself for delivery to my or any eighteenth-century doorstep until such matters of physics are further explored and understood.

Instead, be content with our inter-era correspondence as it is.

And with no cause for trepidation, for despite this demoralized state I will continue to dispense whatever wisdom I possess as to matters of social concern, enmities with men who are fathers by dint of matrimony as opposed to biology, and the relentless pursuits of uniformed constables desiring to mete out punishment for regrettable demeanor displayed while mistakenly believing oneself intoxicated.

I am,
Benjamin Franklin

# CHAPTER 17

Dear Claire Wanzandae,

First of all, I hope you open this letter, but I understand if you don't. I'm already imagining you looking at the return address and dropping it straight into the trash can. But I'm also imagining you reconsidering and digging it back out a few hours later, after it's covered with spaghetti sauce, and cleaning it off and reading these words. I'm not sure where I got that from. It might be in a movie or something.

Second of all, let me say again how sorry I am. I was a jerk and also an idiot on the playground, and I wish I could go back in time and take it all back. Which is actually why I'm writing, because I think maybe I can. But I will get to that in a minute.

# HUGE pain in my ▓▓▓▓!

The hardest part of this last terrible week has not been getting laughed at in the halls or having guys sneak fake vomit into my locker three different times, or even the look of "How Did I Go Wrong in Raising Him?" on my mom's face. It has been the Icy Politeness you have been throwing my way during our Earth Science labs, as if we are distant acquaintances who have never shared a Deep Connection. That's why I have been excusing myself to go to the bathroom so much, and even cut that one class, on Wednesday, if you noticed.

I am not saying any of this to make you feel guilty, Claire Wanzandae. I don't blame you for not wanting to talk to me. I am pretty sick of talking to myself, if you want to know the truth, especially since I have been basically on house arrest for what seems like half my life now, with only my sister among the ranks of those whose opinion of me has not plummeted, and all she really wants to do is play Chutes and Ladders all the time.

So here is what I am going to do, Claire Wanzandae. You are the only one I trust enough to tell. And the only one who won't think I'm crazy. At least, I hope you won't. So here goes.

I have pretty much royally screwed up my existence here in 2015, and I need a fresh start. I need to go someplace where the first words people think when they look at me are not "puker" and "idiot" and "got us busted" and "pretended to be drunk." I need to go somewhere I can feel like a productive member of society, somewhere my Skills can be put to use. Somewhere I can be around a Positive Male Role Model instead of a stepfather who thinks that reading anything longer than the back of a cereal box is a waste of time.

That is why, Claire Wanzandae, I am going to pay a visit to Benjamin Franklin. If pieces of paper can make their way back and forth between our time and his, there is no reason a young Outcast in a cardboard box shouldn't be able to do the same thing. Or maybe there is. I guess I will find out. I have informed Mr. Franklin of my intentions, and he has extended a Hearty Welcome, saying that my presence will be of tremendous help to him and might even have wonderful repercussions on the History of the country.

I am enclosing in this letter a bunch of Old-Time Stamps, and I am hoping that you will use them to write to me, care of BF, at the address I have been using. So that we can stay in Touch, and also so that I can keep tabs on what is happening in the present, because who knows how long I might be busy helping Ben with important Work of a patriotic nature. And if there is anything you Desire from the past, just let me know and I will send it to you if I can. And also, I will be on the constant Lookout for cool things that I think you might like, so don't be surprised if you end up getting a lot of mail and packages containing historical objects of great Value such as original drafts of the Declaration of Independence, for example, though of course that is just an Example because I am writing this from no farther away than my own living room and have no idea if they keep stuff like that lying around to be Snatched Up or what. Maybe I will just send you a dress instead. Who knows, Claire? The possibilities are Endless. Or maybe I should say Beginningless, since we are talking about the past. Just please do not tell anyone where I have gone. Please let that be Our secret.

I hope you know how much I like you, Claire Wanzandae. So much that it hurts my chest to write this. So much that I basically lost my mind trying to act cool and impress you. Hopefully a little time away from all this mess I have made will make me into a better Dude, somebody you can forgive for being such a toolbox, and even want to spend time with again. I don't know when I will see you, but I will be thinking about you, and how your hair always smells like cherry blossoms and gasoline. That is my favorite smell in the world, Claire Wanzandae.

I will say good-bye and Farewell now, because I have to get to work on my Transportation Box. The final thing I want to say is that I have learned from my mistakes, Claire Wanzandae. Especially my mistakes with you and Us. You deserve a guy who can keep his wits about him and treat you like the awesome girl and person you are.

Next time you see me, I am going to be That Guy, Claire. I hope you believe me.

Sincerely Yours in a Conspiracy of Silence (I Hope),
Franklin Isaac Saturday

# CHAPTER 18

Sometimes when you're riding the roller coaster of Bad Luck or even just the Ferris Wheel of Boneheaded Move-Making, the hardest thing in the world is to figure out how to get off. You can shout all you want down at the cigarette-smoking, one-armed carny operating the on/off switch, but that dude can't even hear you over the grinding of machinery, and he probably hates you anyway for having all your own teeth in your mouth. And meanwhile, you just keep turning in circles, or plunging down those terrifying drops, trying to remember what possessed you to get on in the first place.

And if you can't figure it out, your brain starts to get all discombobulated and desperate, and you start trying to make things better by making things worse. It's a lot like when a species of wildlife starts living somewhere it isn't native to and messes up the whole ecosystem.

We learned about this last year in Biology. It's always people's fault. Animals are too smart to go where they aren't supposed to be, but human beings don't think twice about, like, bringing some rare Japanese beetle to Idaho because the colors match the state flag or something. And then—surprise, surprise—the Japanese beetles start eating all the potatoes. So what do the Idahoans do? They bring in a snake native to Mongolia to eat up all the Japanese beetles. And then three months later, the place is overrun with gnarly Mongolian super-snakes that have no natural enemies and don't just enjoy munching on the occasional beetle but also love to devour satellite dishes or small dogs or whatever. So the good people of Idaho put their heads together and conclude that what they need to kill off all the snakes is a goon squad of giant crocodiles.

That was basically the state of mind I was in when I decided to ignore BF's advice and try to mail myself back to 1776. I'd pretty much had it with 2015, and I figured it was time for a brand-new start, or at least a nice, long vacation. Plus, I figured I really could be useful to Ben Franklin and even my Country, seeing as I would be two hundred and thirty-nine years ahead of the game. There had to be some-thing I could invent before it was invented or buy before it was valuable. It would be like playing kickball against a bunch of third graders or something.

So the next day, I cut Earth Science and took the early bus home, and by two twelve, there I was, sitting cross-legged inside a giant cardboard box, with a bottle of water and a smoked turkey and provolone sandwich. I'd written the address on the box, plastered it with all the stamps BF had sent except for the ones I'd mailed to Claire, and then forged a note from my mom to Pat, the mailman, who's this burly, cigar-chomping guy my dad went to high school with, so we're all pretty friendly with him. The note said, *Hi, Pat, this box weighs a ton! Don't even try to lift it without your hand truck! XOXO, K.* And I left it on the curb, right next to our mailbox—although obviously I don't mean "left," since I was inside it with my sandwich and my water. And a tape gun, which I used to seal it up. And an ice pick, which I figured I could use to poke additional holes for breathing if I needed some, though I also made sure to be a little sloppy with the packing tape.

Then I waited. It was super hot in there, which is maybe not surprising, and within about ten minutes I started to rethink the whole thing. The chances of dying started to seem unpleasantly high, between the fact that I was attempting to defy Physics and It might get pissed off and Atomize me, and the likelihood of some simpler but no less deadly box-related mishap, such as getting trapped underneath four hundred other boxes in a hundred-degree mailroom for two days. I started thinking about those monkeys the Russians used to send into space as test cases, and how usually they came back dead and basically never came back with superhuman intelligence, unless the government just covered that part up and is being run by brainiac chimps to this day, which would explain a lot.

I was about a minute away from losing my nerve and busting my way out of the box when I heard the whine of Pat's air brakes, followed by him muttering, "What is she, kidding me?" and sighing. Then nothing for a moment, and then the box tipped sideways as he slid it onto the hand truck, walked the hand truck up the ramp, and dumped the box into his truck.

I ended up lying on my side, and I got kind of drowsy. You might think that a combination of extreme discomfort and heat and fear would keep a person awake, but you would be Wrong. What actually happens, or what happened to me, anyway, is that the body decides to spare you, and it shuts down.

The giant thump of the box hitting the ground woke me up. It felt like I had been dropped onto my butt from a height of about three feet, and I figured that Pat was done with his deliveries and pickups and had just carted me out of the truck and into some kind of sorting room or whatever. There was tinny rock music playing from what sounded like a transistor radio, so I knew I hadn't awakened in the past. Also I could hear voices in the next room talking about the Eagles. The football team, not the National Bird. Or the band, which is, like, Dirk the Jerk's favorite thing to blast around the house on cleaning days and rock out to while he's vacuuming, even though (a) they sound like they all got hit with tranquilizer darts right before they started playing, (b) you can't hear anything when you're vacuuming unless you turn the volume up to one million, which Dirk the Jerk does, and (c) his idea of vacuuming is to move the machine back and forth over one random section of the living room carpet a couple of times on the wrong setting and then go get himself a beer, and basically he could achieve the same results by running a two-by-four over the carpet, because all that happens is it stays dirty, but it gets a stripe on it.

After that, nothing happened for what felt like a hundred years. I ate the sandwich and left the water alone, because the last thing I needed at this point was an uncontrollable urge to pee. I also tried not to think about claustrophobia, because while I was not freaked out, I could kind of feel a freak-out lurking somewhere nearby. I poked a couple of pinholes in my box with the ice pick, and tiny rays of fluorescent light shined their way inside. I pressed my eyeball up against one of the holes and tried to look out. All I could see were other boxes. An ocean of boxes. A few were wrapped in shiny birthday-present paper. None contained a junior high school loser, probably.

Then all the lights went out, and the radio shut off, and I heard voices saying stuff like "Good night, Paulette" and "See ya tomorrow, Lamont."

At that moment, I had an important realization: I was a moron, and if I didn't do something immediately, I was going to be a dead moron in a box. Or, best-case scenario, a very hungry and uncomfortable moron whose mother was going to call 9-1-1 when she got home and found her son missing, then disown him when he was found stowed away in a federal building the next morning. Which, come to think of it, was probably also a serious crime of some kind.

On the other hand, I wasn't especially eager to have Pat or some other random Post Office employee find me trying to mail myself to Ben Franklin with a bunch of two-hundred-year-old stamps for postage, because the last thing I needed on top of being a grounded, thieving liar was to also be considered insane.

I didn't really have the time to slap together an airtight plan, and besides, suddenly I was sweating profusely, that stinky panic-sweat that's totally different from what you get from playing basketball or doing yard work. The whole box filled up with the smell immediately, and before I knew it, I was tearing frantically at the cardboard. I punched my way through the top flaps and nice, cool air poured over me, which was maybe the best feeling of my life.

It didn't last long, because (a) remembering how good it feels to breathe air is one of those things that passes quickly, like being grateful for your health after you're sick, and (b) I still had to announce my illegal and unexplainable presence to Paulette or Lamont or whoever and hope they would be cool about it, which I put at about .001 percent likely.

I yelled "Hey! In here!" as loud as I could. And then, with a sudden flash of non-moronicalness, I ripped off the part of the box with stamps taped to it and shoved it down the front of my pants.

That was when the lights came on.

A pear-shaped lady in a Post Office uniform was standing in the doorway, looking at me with a mix of confusion and concern and fear, like I was a baby Tyrannosaurus rex standing between the cracked halves of my egg or something.

"How did you get in here?" she wanted to know.

"They put me in a box!" I heard myself blurt out. I had no idea what that meant, really, besides that I hadn't put myself in a box, and therefore this wasn't my fault and I shouldn't go to jail or the mental ward for it. So, all things considered, my general reaction was: Nice job, Saturday.

Right away, her face twisted into a look of shock, and she put her hands on her hips. That seemed pretty good.

"Who put you in a box?" she demanded, looking me up and down as if maybe years of Postal Service had conditioned her to automatically judge just how big a box they must have needed.

I took a couple big gulps of air, like maybe I couldn't quite talk yet, and racked my brain for a response.

"The bullies!" is what I came up with. Because everybody hates bullies, right? Nobody is, like, pro-bully. And also, bullies are a hot topic right now. Granted, stuffing a kid inside a box and mailing him is pretty extreme bullying behavior, and also pretty old-timey, since nowadays bullying more often takes the form of putting mean posts up on somebody's Facebook page, but maybe Post Office Paulette didn't know that, since she was pretty old.

"What bullies?" she said, taking a step closer to me. "Are you all right?"

I figured the smart thing to do was focus on the second question and ignore the first.

"I think so. Can I have some water?" I said, and when Paulette turned to go get me some, I followed her out of the sorting room, stepping on about a dozen boxes in the process and probably mashing a couple of very thoughtful gifts into a fine paste.

In the hallway was a water cooler, and when she turned around with a paper cone full of *agua* for me, I was right behind her and Paulette went "Aaah!" and dropped the cone on the floor, then touched her palm to her chest and said, "You startled me."

"Sorry," I said, and then tried to dodge past her. I could see the front room, just down the hall, and the street outside. From the light, it looked like it was about six o'clock, which meant that Mom and Dirk the Jerk were both back from work and wondering where I was, particularly since I was mega-ultra-super-grounded and under strict orders to come directly home the minute school ended.

Paulette stepped to her right and blocked me. "Where do you think you're going?" she asked.

"I've got to get home," I said. "My parents are probably worried sick."

She shook her head. "Oh no. We've got to file a police report. That's a crime, what they did. A *federal* crime."

"I don't want to press charges," I told her, which was a line straight off of every TV show ever made.

"It doesn't matter what you want," Paulette said, furrowing her brow at me. "Rules are rules." And she half turned and picked up a phone mounted to the wall.

"Please," I said, moving back in front of her and making my eyes as wide and puppy-dog-like as possible. "Just— you'll make it worse. I'm begging you, just let me go home."

Paulette gave me a long stare, super deadpan, and then hung up the phone. "All right," she said at last. "No police. But I'm sure as heck not letting you just disappear into the night, either. We're calling your parents."

"Okay," I said, nodding like I was super grateful as my

HUGE pain in my ~~███~~!

armpits dampened with massive quantities of gross fear-sweat. "Thank you."

I was already wondering if I was going to be able to make the bully story fly once Pat the mailman got wind of this incident—which he definitely would, it seemed to me, since Ike in a Box was probably the most exciting thing to happen at the local post office since the debut of the Fat Elvis stamp. I was also going to have to figure out why and how the bullies had boxed me up right in front of my own house. Maybe they'd coerced me into telling them my mother's name, and the name of our mailman?

Also, I was going to need at least two fake bullies. With phone numbers, since my mother was not going to rest until she'd talked to their parents. I wondered if I could give her Ryan Demphill's cell number, and whether Ryan's older sister could pass as one of the bullies' moms. Maybe the bullies could be brothers, so I only needed one mom?

The knot in my stomach told me that the answer to at least one of these questions was probably no.

# CHAPTER 19

The first big warning sign of just how deep a hole I'd dug myself was that Dirk the Jerk was the one who picked me up from the Post Office. Every once in a while, my mom kind of throws up her hands in frustration and makes him take over—with Carolyn if she's in a super-difficult mood, or the trash disposal if it starts shooting chopped-up garbage into the air, or me if we're locked into one of those Why/Because I Said So/But Why–type conversations. Deep down she knows that handing the reins over to the Jerk will only make things worse and fifteen minutes later she'll have to take over again, except maybe with the trash disposal. It's less of a problem-solving strategy than a sign that she's reached her limit.

As soon as I saw the Jerkmobile pull up, I started getting angry. After all, I'd supposedly just spent the afternoon being terrorized by bullies, and instead of showing up to comfort me, my mom sends him? What was up with that?

"Who did this?" he demanded the second I closed the door. "How did it happen?"

The way Dirk the Jerk said it was the exact opposite of sympathetic, like what he really meant was *How are you such a loser that you ended up in a box?* And that made me so angry that without really thinking it all the way through, I ditched my whole strategy of pathetic victimhood, which had some pretty big flaws in it anyway, and went in a whole other direction.

I watched Paulette walk back inside the Post Office and sighed a long, dramatic sigh as a way to buy myself a couple of seconds and decide whether I was crazy to say what I was about to say.

On one hand, I was about to toss my alibi in the Dumpster and put myself on the hook for a boneheaded act of Federal lawbreaking. But on the other hand, at least now I wouldn't have to make up any fake bullies. And besides, how much more trouble could I be in, anyway? You can't add anything to infinity.

"It was a dare," I said. "Me and some of my buddies were messing around, and they dared me to ship myself across town, so I did."

*Yeah,* I thought. *Take that, Dirk the Jerk.* I have buddies who are cool, and we dare each other to do crazy stuff because we're awesome like that. Whereas you have nothing but a couple of stamp-collector bozo acquaintances you see once every three months for half-priced drinks at Houlihan's.

Dirk the Jerk shook his head and did this snort-type laugh that sounded like an insult in itself, and said, "You're a piece of work, kid."

He had never called me kid before, as far as I could remember. That felt like an insult, too. In fact, the whole sentence felt like something he would never say in front of my mom. Maybe he had come to get me so we could have some kind of private man-to-Jerk conversation.

"So are you," I said back.

Dirk the Jerk's jaw rippled, like he was grinding his teeth together with the effort of not getting pulled into my childish game of name-calling, even though he had started it.

"Look," he said after a minute, and stopped at a red light and turned to look at me. "I was twelve once, too, okay?"

"I'm thirteen," I said.

The light turned green.

"It's green," I pointed out.

"Don't tell me how to drive," Dirk the Jerk said, but he hit the gas hard, and we lurched forward.

"Good talk," I said.

Dirk the Jerk ignored that and kept driving, and after a while I felt bad because maybe this really was his Big Moment of trying to connect with me, so I said, "What were you like when you were thirteen?"

"A lot cooler than you," he said, and turned on the radio.

It turns out that you can add on to infinity after all.

My mom was sitting on the couch, reading a book to Carolyn, when me and Dirk the Jerk walked in. All she said was "Dinner's in five. Go wash up. Caro, go with him."

Carolyn jumped to her feet and took my hand. I tried to hear what Mom and the Jerk were talking about from the bathroom, but between the running water and Carolyn entertaining me with spontaneously invented knock-knock jokes that made no sense, I couldn't make out more than a couple of words, such as *dare* and *criminal*. But by the time we sat down at the table, my mom had borrowed Claire Wanzandae's gradually-turning-into-a-statue look, and everything she said during the meal was short and clipped, like she'd trimmed each sentence with gardening shears.

I figured I was in for another teary conversation about trust and honesty and disappointment once Caro was in bed, and I spent the whole evening dreading it but also wishing we could get it over with, like a prisoner waiting in his cell for a trial he knows he can't win. But that wasn't what happened. When Mom came back from tucking Carolyn in, she and Dirk the Jerk stood next to each other to form a United Front and all she did was read my sentence. That was even worse, because (a) it felt like she'd given up on me, and (b) the sentence.

The sentence went like this: Not only was I grounded even more indefinitely than before, but also: no phone, not even answering it if it rings. No TV. No Internet, no video games, no board games, no doing anything after school except homework and "thinking about my choices." On weekends until further notice, I would be helping the Jerk with various home-improvement projects such as cleaning the gutters, painting the fence, maybe breaking a few boulders with a pickax while wearing a black-and-white-striped uniform.

It was the board game part that really chilled me to the core. I mean, taking away a guy's main sources of recreation, like seeing friends and watching movies, that was one thing.

But taking the time to specifically prohibit something like board games, which I only play as a "family activity" or out of extreme boredom or to entertain Carolyn—that was cold-blooded for real. She might as well have asked me if there was anything else I enjoyed in the world that she had mistakenly overlooked.

"What about Dad?" was all I could think to say, once I'd taken it all in.

"Oh, he'll hear about this," my mom said, crossing her arms, which she had just finished uncrossing.

"No, I mean, can I call him?"

From the looks on their faces, they hadn't thought about that. "We'll discuss it," Mom said. I wasn't sure if she meant her and me, or her and the Jerk, or maybe even her and my dad. But I knew better than to ask. And anyway, it wasn't like the occasional awkward phone call with my dad was going to provide much relief, as far as this punishment was concerned.

That night I lay in my bed and stared at the ceiling, which is covered in these dumb glow-in-the-dark star stickers I'd put up there when I was Caro's age that are impossible to scrape off and will probably be the main artifact of our civilization to survive and be studied by archaeologists of the distant future. Tomorrow was Saturday and Monday was some teacher-training holiday, which meant I had three full days of getting bossed around by a beer-drinking Dirk the Jerk while standing on a ladder with my hands covered in leaf gunk to look forward to. That would at least keep my mind off the fact that Claire Wanzandae was probably at the movies with some lacrosse player right now, and that at least two hundred jokes had been made at my expense within her earshot tonight, and possibly she had even made one or two of them herself, and ditto Ryan Demphill.

Then it occurred to me that Claire was probably grounded herself, and so was Ryan. That made me feel slightly better.

Until I remembered that they both probably blamed me for it, which made me feel slightly worse than I had to begin with.

I lay there staring at those stupid stars for two or three hours, trying to find a ray of hope.

The last thing I remember thinking before I finally fell asleep was: at least Mom didn't ground me from the Sending and Receiving of letters.

# CHAPTER 20

Dear Franklin—

My father, by trade, was a Boston candle maker. His shop had a blue ball hanging over the entry boasting to all in want of light that, in the rear of those quarters, cow and sheep fat were melted into tallow, which was poured into a mold and, upon cooling, were capable of providing illumination. I often helped him after my day at the Boston Latin School was over. And at night, I returned home, where I read books by the light of the crooked candles he could not sell.

Though my father was a man of piety in possession of devout religious and child-rearing conviction, because I was the fifteenth of the seventeen children for whom he and his second wife, Abiah, were responsible, he had been rendered exhausted by the time of my youth. Perhaps it was that relaxation of order that allowed me the liberty to manifest self-discipline. And to question the motivations of those in authority with a penchant for oppression.

By way of illustration, I allude to my older brother James, a printer for whom I served as an apprentice upon his founding of the *New-England Courant*—oft regarded as the first truly independent periodical within our thirteen colonies. During my indentured servitude, James denied my desire for publication by virtue of my younger age. Rather than accede, however, I defied his edict by proceeding to write letters of a satirical nature under the pseudonym Mrs. Silence Dogood that soon became the subject of conversation about town. Yet, upon eventual detection of the ruse, James grew incensed, ceased further publication of my letters, and, to the very day he passed from this life, he uttered not a single word to me.

I submit this biographical précis, young Franklin, for purposes of drawing comparison to our respective proclivities. Whether a man's makeup is a genetic

# HUGE pain in my ▓▓▓!

disposition or attributable to postnatal influences is a matter for others to debate. I have neither the time nor the desire. But upon empirical consideration of manifested behavior, my inference, by dint of this ongoing correspondence, is that we share a penchant for inquiry, a propensity for adventure, and a paucity of patience. Our differences, however, are most dramatically disparate. For whereas I espy the horizons and endeavor to fill their voids, you, on the contrary, create voids where unnecessary and then commit to recklessly fill them with absolute disregard to logic, nor even the most remote semblance of Sanity.

In this particular instance, it was in the form of a letter I discovered in my postal receptacle upon return from still another most harrowing day with the Committee of Five. A session that found me in receipt of a churn full of insults upon learning that Thomas Jefferson of Virginia had taken a most handsome French vase I had given him after my latest return from Paris—a gift presented with the most sincere intentions despite my disdain for him—and given it to his sister as a housewarming gift when visiting her new home in Alexandria. At first, my instinct was to grant benefit of doubt as this was conveyed to me by John Adams of Massachusetts, who claimed to have seen it last weekend at Jefferson's sister's house, yet is prone to misidentification because of his vain refusal to don a pair of the bifocals I invented. However, his observation was subsequently verified by both Robert Sherman of Connecticut and Robert Livingston of New York, as I learned that all three of my distinguished colleagues saw Jefferson carrying the vase into the festive gathering to which I was not invited.

"Where were you?" Jefferson queried upon my arrival at the Second Continental Congress this morning. "Your absence at my sister's new home was duly noticeable."

"I did not know about it, Thomas Jefferson of Virginia, for I did not receive an invitation."

"But I assure you that I sent one, Benjamin Franklin of Pennsylvania. Must have gotten lost in the mail. You know how poorly run our postal system is," he uttered as if unaware that I had invented that selfsame system.

So I was already in a piqued mood when I withdrew

my mail and sorted through it. On any given day, I receive, in approximation, a dozen posted articles per delivery. For the most part, they consist of bills. One of this lot's was from the gentleman whom I contracted to clean the Franklin Stove that I invented. My initial reaction was, "Had I not given existence to this very stove, this man would not have a business. So, as a gesture of appreciation, should he not clean my Franklin Stove free of charge?"

Therefore my temperament was becoming more frayed when I came upon an envelope that was addressed to you, "Franklin Isaac Saturday," in care of me, "Benjamin Franklin," at my home address, "316 Market Street, Philadelphia, Pennsylvania." The return address informed that the letter was sent by a Miss Claire Wanzandae, whose name I recognized as the elaborately tressed object of your affectionate stirrings.

Just why you would have anyone send a letter to me, at my home, in the year I exist, implies only one thing—that you are scheming to act on your expressed desire to come here and to cross my doorstep, in spite of my emphatic admonishments to the contrary. Perhaps you have already arrived and are roaming the streets of Colonial Philadelphia as if there were not already sufficient unrest in my fair city. If you are indeed here, I implore you to mail yourself back. If you are planning to come, I implore you to stay put. There is no void here that you need to fill. More to my point, there is no void here you need to fill with you.

In an attempt to accentuate my most fervent conviction concerning this matter, I am mailing back Claire Wanzandae's letter to you, unopened, at your address, in your century. Again, if you are currently here, you now have little choice but to post yourself back so you can read it. And if you are still there, let it provide incentive for you to remain there, read it, discuss its contents with Claire Wanzandae, and continue to remain there.

I am,
Benjamin Franklin

P.S. Did I mention that you should remain there?

# CHAPTER 21

Dear Ike,

I'm really hoping that you came to your senses and did not do this thing. That you did not get inside a box and mail yourself to 1776. But I have not seen you or been able to get in touch for five days now, and you are falling way behind in Earth Science and History, and I am feeling extremely concerned. I've called your house and gotten the answering machine twice and your little sister once. I tried to ask her where you were, but all she said was "Ikey can never talk to anyone again," which scared me even more. I also tried to e-mail you, but no response.

If I have not heard from you by tomorrow, I am going to take the bus over to your house. I am crossing my fingers that you will come to the door in your pajamas, all sneezy and congested. But I would not bet on it. I would so much not bet on it that I'm actually feeling sick to my stomach right now. Maybe you are not the only one prone to puking for stupid reasons.

I feel really bad about the way I have been treating you, Ike. And I'm ashamed that it took you disappearing to make me say so. Especially since I have watched everybody else be so mean to you and blame you for getting them busted like they didn't decide to sneak out of their houses to begin with. I should not have let you go through all that alone. And the truth is, I'm not even mad at you anymore. I just didn't know how to stop acting like I was, as dumb as that probably sounds.

At first, sure, I was super annoyed. Not even so much at getting barfed on, though I could definitely live my whole life without getting barfed on again and have no regrets about it. But what really made me mad was seeing you act not like yourself. It was super weird and kind of upsetting to see you try to impress me by being more like everybody else. Like all the regular, jerky boys.

# HUGE pain in my ▓▓▓▓!

And if I really think about it, Ike, the reason that made me so mad is: why would you think you needed to be someone else for me? Because I like you for who you are. For being different. And sweet. And funny. And cute.

I like you a lot, Ike. If I didn't, I would not have been so disappointed. And my stomach wouldn't be hurting right now from the thought of you taping yourself inside a box and mailing yourself to Ben Franklin.

You don't need to change, Ike. Not for me. You just need to come home. I'm sure Benjamin Franklin can manage on his own. According to our history books, he did just fine without you there.

I will be waiting for you, Ike.


See you soon (I hope),
Claire Wanzandae


P.S.—I have been meaning to tell you I like how you always say my whole name, Franklin Isaac Saturday. I never used to like my name, but now I do.

# CHAPTER 22

The first thing I did when I read the letter from Claire Wanzandae inside the letter from B-Freezy was leap out of bed and wriggle my way out of my bathrobe and start looking for some decent clothes. I had been home sick all week, which was why Claire hadn't seen me, but when I read those words of Devotion and Apology, I felt strong enough to bench-press a horse. Or at least ride my bike over to Claire's house and present myself in Person, even if that meant getting regrounded until the age of forty-five.

Then I sneezed so hard that stars danced around my head like in an old-timey cartoon, and I sat back down on my mattress.

The reason I was sick was that it had rained all day Sunday. Normally, that would not make a person sick, because a person would be inside. But not this person, because in his capacity as New Family Disciplinarian, Dirk the Jerk had forced this person to clean the gutters anyway and also do a bunch of other yard work. He and my mom had a fight about it, with her taking the part of Reason and saying stuff like "He'll get sick," and Dirk the Jerk taking the part of Jerk and responding with such timeless pearls of wisdom as "He's gotta learn" and "Come on, Kristin, a little rain never hurt anybody." Which was easy for him to say because he spent the afternoon sitting on the couch, watching the Phillies game, which was a very rain-free environment and also did not feature Driving Winds such as I experienced up on my rickety ladder.

So I spent the school holiday in bed, which is the ultimate bummer for any kid of school-going age, and then I missed Tuesday and Wednesday as well. Being sick was better than going to school, though, and while I was beginning to feel better, I was also wondering if I could milk it for a couple more days—or even through the weekend so as to avoid further Hard Labor. My mother had relented and allowed me to watch TV while convalescing, despite my punishment, so I was sitting pretty for a kid whose life is ruined. Plus, Dirk the Jerk was in the doghouse for getting me sick, which helped to ease my pain.

But Claire Wanzandae's letter did more than ease my pain. It unruined my life times a million, and the thought of her sitting in her room, fretting about me, was more than I could bear.

I had to see her. I had to look her in the eye and start in on my promise of being Better. We had a whole Life in front of us, and I wasn't going to screw it up again. I could feel it in my bones: a kind of soaring, ticklish feeling like you get sometimes when you're riding in a really fast elevator, only this time it meant A Brand-New Start and A Brand-New Ike.

Then another thought hit me. Not only was I going to be better, I was going to make the World better. Sometimes all a guy needs is the right girl by his Side, and he can accomplish anything. Especially if he has access to a great man of the past and can Influence the very shaping of the country through Wise Counsel.

That idea made me even more excited, and I stood up again and rummaged around until I found a pair of pants that weren't too dirty and pulled them on. Then I sneezed six times in a row, which was a personal record, and decided that maybe I should just concentrate all my energy on getting Well and see Claire in school tomorrow, since getting her sick was not exactly the most chivalrous Move.

I woke up the next day fully recovered and feeling like it was Christmas instead of just Thursday, from the anticipation of seeing Claire Wanzandae. I asked Mom to drive me to school early so that I could meet with my teachers before classes started and get caught up on the work I'd missed, which sounded very impressive to her, and she was happy to do it. But of course that was totally bogus, and really I just wanted to catch Claire, who goes to school early twice a week for Latin, which is this stepchild-type class that's not important enough to be held during regular school hours. Kids basically get forced to take it because their parents think it will help them on their SATs five years from now, since a lot of words come from Latin. Which seems pretty stupid to me, since way more words come from Reading.

I had a picture in my mind of how the big reunion with Claire was going to go. I was going to post up on the steps outside school, real cool and kind of brooding, and she'd be walking with a friend and all of a sudden look up and see me and say "Oh my god!" and run into my arms and start crying and say "I thought I'd lost you," and then I'd say "I'm back," and she'd blink away her tears and kiss me.

Which is probably how it would have gone except that my mom watched me from the car until I went inside, the way she'd watch one of my friends she was dropping off at home to make sure he got into his house. So I had no choice but to linger in the lobby, examining all the dusty art projects on display inside the glass cases on the walls, which nobody had ever looked at before in the entire history of the world. And somehow I failed to intercept Claire Wanzandae on her way to Latin and instead had to wander the halls until I found the classroom, then stand outside it like a goon, trying to get her attention through the little window in the door.

I couldn't even see Claire through that window, but I could see Marcy Wong, who was Claire's friend, and so I mouthed *Claire* at her and jabbed my finger in a motion that was meant to convey the concept of: *Get her to come out here.*

Marcy Wong gave me a look of: *You could not be any grosser to me if you had a booger hanging out of your nose right now.* But a couple of minutes later, the door opened and out stepped Claire Wanzandae, and her pretty brown eyes lit up when she saw me, and without even saying a word, she threw her arms around my neck and gave me this huge hug.

It's possible that I have felt better in my life than I did at that moment, but it's also possible that I have not.

"I've been so worried about you," she whispered once the hug ended, which was several awesome seconds later.

"I'm okay," I said. "I didn't go. I just got sick."

"I was sure you had," Claire said. "I sent you a letter."

"I know," I told her. "Ben sent it to me." And I slipped it out of my pocket to show her. "He told me to pass along his kind regards."

Claire stared at it for a moment. Then she spoke really slowly. "Ben...Franklin...held...my...letter. *The* Ben Franklin."

She kind of shook her head clear, which made her hair shimmer in a magical-type way beneath the fluorescent lights of the hallway, and said, "I guess it's just kind of hitting me how incredible this is."

"I know," I said. "That's why we've got to make the most of it. I've been thinking. I've had a lot of time to think, these last few days." I took her hand, like that was no big deal, and said, "We can help him, Claire. Me and you. We can make this country better. From the very beginning."

She let me hold on to her hand, but her face got a little darker, like a cloud had passed over the fluorescent lights, and said, "What do you mean?"

"We know all kinds of stuff. I mean, think about it—what if, like, the polio vaccine had been invented a hundred years earlier? Thousands of lives would have been saved. Or if somebody had told Abraham Lincoln not to go to that play—he never would have been assassinated!"

Claire was shaking her head back and forth very fast now.

"Uh-uh, Ike. No way. You don't mess with the past. Everybody knows that."

"But we can make the world a better place!"

"But how do we know what will happen? Let's say somebody warns Lincoln not to go to that play. So he lives, great. But then the next night, he cooks himself a steak. And so the butcher sells one more steak that night than he was supposed to. And the last steak of the day, the one he wouldn't even have sold, has something wrong with it, so the person who buys it gets sick and goes home, instead of going out and meeting the girl he was supposed to marry. What if that person is my great-great-great-great-grandfather? Then I'd never exist."

"Why would the president of the United States be cooking for himself?"

"That's not the point and you know it."

It wasn't, and I did. But I also wasn't ready to give up on this idea. It had too much Meaning. And how does any Good get done if there isn't also Risk?

"Okay," I said. "You're right. But it's too late—we've already messed with the past by writing to Ben, so we might as well try to make the most of it. What if we can prevent a tragedy or something, Claire? Isn't it worth it to try? Isn't it wrong *not* to try?"

Claire stood quietly for a while. I waited and listened to the muffled sound of nerds conjugating Latin verbs. I could tell she was turning it over in her mind. The idea of it being wrong not to try had definitely made an impact on her. Claire Wanzandae is a very moral person.

"We need to talk to someone who knows way more about history than us," she decided.

And that is how Claire Wanzandae and I ended up spending our lunch period in Mr. Larrapin's room, watching him munch on a weird peanut butter and lettuce sandwich he claimed was delicious and asking him questions such as "If you could go back in time and tell the guys writing the Declaration of Independence anything, what would it be and why?" while pretending that our sudden fascination with Colonial America was totally random and our desire to spend our only free time talking about it with him was supremely normal.

"Hmm," said Mr. Larrapin, wiping his mouth on a paper towel and then taking a drink from a thermos containing what smelled like peppermint tea. "This is going to sound like a really boring answer, but what I'd really want to do is show them a map."

"That is a really boring answer," I said without thinking, and Claire gave me a little slap on the arm.

"Why, Mr. Larrapin?" she asked.

Mr. Larrapin stood up, brushed some crumbs off his shirt, and pulled down his trusty gigantic Map o' America.

"Here are the thirteen colonies," he said, running a finger down the eastern seaboard. "Notice anything?"

"Yeah," I said. "They're like one-twentieth of the country."

"That's right. They were all clustered together like that because those guys had no real idea how big the continent was. They didn't have a firm grasp on how the coastline looked, or where the bodies of water were, or even how far one town was from another. They were fighting a guerilla war, and they won it, but their understanding of the geography was very limited. Very local. One look at a decent map would have been tremendously helpful—it might have shortened the war by months, or even years. But, of course, there was no such thing as a decent map, back then."

I thought that over. Sending BF a map seemed like exactly the kind of low-risk, morally important Move we could make. I started to get excited thinking about it. One trip to a gas station, and we would be Patriots and Heroes. Then my mind started to wander, and next thing I knew, I was thinking about all the other things at a modern gas station that would be Mind-Blowing to B-Freezy, such as Chili Cheese Fritos and four-month-old hot dogs rotating slowly under a heat lamp and forty-eight-ounce fountain sodas that would rot every tooth in your head and probably dissolve the wooden dentures they had back in His day, too.

Also, cars.

I snapped out of it and decided to make sure I understood what Mr. Larrapin was saying, because it was pretty Monumental.

"So with a modern map, they could've won the war faster?"

Mr. Larrapin nodded. "I'd say so, yes."

"Saving millions of lives?"

He laughed. "Thousands, anyway."

"That's still a lot," I pointed out pointlessly.

"What else?" Claire asked.

Mr. Larrapin yanked the map, and it rolled back up into its little coil at the top of the blackboard. "Well, one fascinating thing about the Declaration of Independence is that for many years after it was written, it was a relatively obscure document. It was written for a specific purpose, and once it fulfilled that purpose, it wasn't until Lincoln quoted it in the Gettysburg Address that it gained the iconic status it has today. Now, that's not to say that it hadn't been influential in terms of providing a template for other colonies, particularly the assertion of the right to revolution...."

Mr. Larrapin then proceeded to drone on for another twenty-three uninterrupted minutes, touching on such topics as what the British thought about the role of Parliamentary power in the colonies, how Paul Revere didn't really go on his famous ride and actually some poet made all that up years later, and how until pretty late in the game most colonists were in favor of working out their differences with England, not going to war.

HUGE pain in my ████!

It was the usual teacherly mix of interesting and boring, but none of it was relevant to our secret Purpose except the map. That's usually the way it is when you ask grown-ups a question: the useful part of their answer is almost always the first thirty seconds, but you have to stand there, watching their lips move and going "uh-huh, uh-huh, uh-huh" for twenty times that long.

Finally, Claire made some kind of excuse about needing to get her gym clothes from her locker, and we got out of there. Mr. Larrapin waved good-bye to us with his sandwich, the lettuce flopping out between the bread like a wide green tongue, and told us to come back any time. Man, that guy was lonely.

"Map?" I said once the door closed behind us. The word echoed through the empty hallway.

"Map," Claire Wanzandae said back, like we were talking in a secret code. And she took out her notebook.

# CHAPTER 23

Dear Ben,

This letter is not just from me but also from Claire Wanzandae, which ought to give you some Indication that things are much better in my Realm than they were the last time I wrote. You are a good friend for helping me through that rough patch I got myself into through Moronic Acts, and I have been giving a lot of thought to how I could repay the favor of your Solid advice.

But not just repay it, Ben Franklin. Sometimes in the course of human events it becomes necessary for a Kid to make a Difference. That is why this is more than a mere letter. It is a care package. From Ike and Claire to The Republic Itself. After much thought and also consultation with Wise Experts, we have decided that it is our solemn duty to contribute to the war effort by offering you the benefit of Future Knowledge. Therefore, you will find enclosed in this Package:

1. Several maps, intended to provide you with a better understanding of the country's size, shape, and terrain so that you can better fight the British and hopefully win the war Quickly and Efficiently, with a minimum of blood Spilled on both sides. There is one of Pennsylvania, one of Massachusetts, one of New England, and one of the whole country.

The Fifty States, BF. We know that is probably a Brain-Melting concept, but it is what happens. This land is your land, Ben Franklin. This land is my land. From California (which does not exist yet) to the New York island (which is an island, as you probably figured out already). From the Redwood forest (which is in what will someday be California) to the Gulf Stream waters (which are not land at all, obviously). This land was made for you and me. That whole thing is a quote from a song by Woody Guthrie that Claire Wanzandae's dad likes, BF, but do not try to Claim it as your own invention, because Woody Guthrie is going to be cool when he is Born.

2. Speaking of claiming stuff, we are also enclosing a diagram, drawn by Claire, explaining the simple but amazing concept of: The Sandwich. We have spent a long time discussing what Information is either so crucial to the Country that we have no choice but to give it, or else so Impossible to Cause Damage that it is Okay to Tell. And that is how we came up with the sandwich, because the sandwich is delicious and has only made the world a better place, and also it seems to us like a perfect Feather in your cap of Inventions. Especially if you hurry, because soon it is going to be invented and named by the Earl of Sandwich over in London. So that is another reason: to rob the enemy of their Greatest Accomplishment. We only have one request, which is that you call it not the Sandwich but the Claireike, which is obviously a better name. The Claireike is not only tasty, nutritious, and versatile (as you can see from the list of Popular Claireikes jotted next to the diagram) but also a great food for Times of War or even just Activity, because it is highly portable.

# HUGE pain in my ▓▓▓▓!

3. Finally, we are also enclosing, for your Delectation, one actual peanut butter and jelly Claireike, made by Claire and Ike.

So there you have it, BF: some tools for Victory and Satisfaction. You do not have to thank us, because we are just doing our Duty as citizens and friends. We will eagerly await word concerning the Impact our contribution makes, though of course it is up to you, in your Wisdom, to decide whether to use this stuff at all and, if so, how. We understand that you can't very well just stroll into the next Committee of Five meeting and say, "Hey, look, some maps," but surely there is some Slick way to go about it, especially since people are already used to you Inventing something every time their backs are turned. Plus, you will buy their Goodwill and Support the second you distribute that first round of Claireikes. Not even Jefferson will be immune to their Charm—trust us.

Your Friends in Liberty,
Ike and Claire

# CHAPTER 24

Sometimes the biggest difference in the world is between doing a thing alone and doing that same thing not alone. For example, watching a football game alone is whatever. Decent. Not great, not terrible, but pretty all right and maybe straight-up enjoyable if you have the right Snacks. But watching that same exact football game with Dirk the Jerk sucks so much that if you could harness that suckiness in the form of pure energy, you could power the state of Colorado for a week.

Waiting for BF to write back by myself was boring and nervous-making at the same time. But waiting with Claire was like being cuddled up around a secret together. Like we'd just bought a puppy no one else could see and we were quietly petting it and feeding it treats. Although

HUGE pain in my ▓▓▓▓!

I guess if we had an invisible puppy, people would wonder why we were constantly crouched over, petting the air, and also how all those dog biscuits were magically disappearing, and probably we'd end up in jail or being studied by a team of government scientists at an undisclosed location or something.

Anyway, my point is that after we sent that letter, I felt pretty much invincible. Claire and I were a team now. A united front, except unlike Mom and Dirk the Jerk we weren't united against anything, we were just united in a feeling of Closeness. Everybody knew it, too, because Claire Wanzandae and I held hands sometimes in the hallway now. And I didn't even care. That people knew, I mean. Because that didn't matter. I thought it did, back before I knew what a Relationship really was, but now I knew how dumb and immature that thought had been. Like when Claire came to my house that first day and I was so into having everybody see us together on the bus and even touched her back to guide her toward a seat like Claire Wanzandae had just arrived from some remote village in Papua New Guinea and had never been on a bus before. That was as embarrassing to think back on now as the Playground Incident. Or almost, anyway. Both of them were the same thing, really. Ike not being in touch with his True Self and consequently acting like a bozo of gigantic proportions.

But all that was behind me now. I had a good woman by my side and also a Mission, and any day now we were going to receive a letter confirming the great contributions we had made to American History, and maybe those contributions would even ripple forward through the Space-Time Continuum, and one day we'd wake up in a world where there were no longer any such things as sandwiches, but the Claireike was a lunchtime staple, and the two of us would have a little private chuckle that lasted for the rest of our lives.

I had started walking Claire home from school every day, partly out of Chivalry but mostly because we had put her return address on the last letter. It turned out there was a city bus that I could take from kind of near her house to semi near mine, so no more hoofing six miles home or having to turn right around to make it back to school in time for the sports bus. Plus, the mail got delivered earlier in her neighborhood than in mine, which meant we had a way better chance of being together to get the letter this way.

On the day it finally came, we had been doing this thing of pretending we weren't thinking about the letter, which ended up working so well that by the time we got to her house, both of us had actually forgotten about it. We were talking about Mr. Larrapin, actually. Specifically, the question of whether he was married and, as an auxiliary question, who would possibly marry a guy like that. Claire said he didn't wear a wedding ring, but that her Uncle Lou, who was married, also didn't wear a wedding ring, and so that didn't prove anything. I asked her if she thought that maybe Uncle Lou didn't wear a wedding ring because he preferred people and, in particular, ladies to think he was single, but Claire shook her head and said it was just because Uncle Lou was a rebel.

Then we reached Claire's house and remembered that we'd been pretending not to think about the mail and opened the mailbox and found a letter that changed everything and also made me throw up in my mouth a little bit. But not really, because that's just an expression kids at school are using now.

# CHAPTER 25

Dear Ike and Claire Wanzandae—

As I sit here placing quill to paper, my most idle thoughts stray to Francis Folger Franklin.

After an historic session with the Committee marked by turns that not even I could have predicted, I am taking a well-deserved respite in a local tavern called the Tavern, which is located down the street from the print shop that is producing copies of the Declaration of Independence for distribution among my fellow colonists. A quiet, simple celebration over a potpie, which is a specialty here at the Tavern.

Francis was my first son born in wedlock. Deborah and I called him Franky and he was a golden child—his smiles brighter, his babblings more telling, and his tricks more magical than all the other infants in the colonies combined. When he was born, I could not believe that such elation was humanly possible. And until the Lord chose to reclaim him from us when he was but four, I was unaware that the human heart could know such pain.

It is a throbbing that lingers silently to this day and renders me prone to frequent bouts of melancholia. It is the very reason that, in contrast to my repute as a jaunty bon vivant about town, I am a rather private man who prefers the quiet solemnity of home. My sanctuary. A haven where I arise at dawn, peruse the periodicals in the warmth of an unmade bed, then sketch ideas for new inventions after a solitary breakfast. And upon my return at day's end, having left the tumult inherent in dealing with others, I delight in reentering my home, where I soothe myself in a lengthy bath; exit to the yard, where I tend to my garden; reenter my home to take another lengthy bath to remove any soil now clinging to my body resultant from tending to my garden; dine alone; then inscribe the events or thoughts of that day into this journal or lose myself in the musings of a favorite author until I reach the edge of sleep.

I am, if not old, then older. At this juncture, I prefer changes to take wide turns, as opposed to the jolts that excite younger men. And so I embrace my time-honored routine, as it provides comfort in an otherwise unpredictable existence.

By way of consequence, I am a man governed by habit. I take pride in my resistance to deviation. To that end, all that I possess has a rightful place, with my full expectation that it be there when reached for. Though my home boasts more than adequate illumination by dint of lamps that represent the cutting edge in whale oil-fueled technology, I most faithfully presume that all objects will be in their proper spheres of assignation lest I seek them in a darkened room.

Yet today, at this moment, as if magically, I harken back to the time of Franky's birth and delight in saying that my current spirit is on the precipice of revisiting that jubilation. For we are conjuring change with an optimism capable of nullifying all that threatens, and we shall expel even the slightest hint of darkness with verve as we forge ahead upon our crucial mission.

I love our thirteen colonies, Ike and Claire Wanzandae. And the possibilities of independence. And equality. And I embrace the pride I feel at the very sound of the words *the United States of America*.

Therefore, as I consume yet another forkful of yet a second potpie, I reflect back on the day that preceded this repast. At the meeting of the Second Continental Congress, where I arrived with a hop to my stride and the contents of your package under my fleshy arm.

"Pray tell, what is this outrageous doggerel?" queried Thomas Jefferson of Virginia.

"*Fifty* states?" exclaimed Roger Sherman of Connecticut.

I had unfurled the map you sent me onto the floor and anchored it by standing upon two opposite corners and placing my tricornered hat and the bronze bust of Jefferson that he insists on bringing with him every day, as if one image of him in such confined quarters wasn't enough, on the other two.

"Yes, fifty states!" I responded with an excitement I assumed would be infectious. Yet, to my greatest dismay, I found myself at the outset of this historic meeting a committee of one versus a committee of four. "Our country's potential is far greater than any of us could possibly have conceived."

"And why is that?" asked Robert Livingston of New York with an inflection that was either inquisitive or derisive.

"Making the thirteen colonies fifty states does not change the amount of land they occupy, just as dividing a rhubarb pie into fifty slices does not make it larger than dividing it into thirteen slices," he deemed fit to add. And by virtue of this addition, I made a final determination that his query was inquisitive, as he was apparently far too mentally deficient to be derisive.

"Our nation-to-be possesses a far greater expanse of land than we ever fathomed," I bellowed while straddling its borders. "Observe," I demanded, and directed them to note that even my rather substantial undercarriage, hovering above the map, could not cover the entire territory from sea to shining sea. Or, in this particular instance, from hip to swaying hip.

"Not to mention these two other future states," I said, pointing to the masses labeled *Alaska* and *Hawaii* and inset in boxes in the middle of what appeared to be an ocean beyond the western border.

"And just where did you get this map?" asked John Adams of Massachusetts.

"Yes, where?" parroted Roger Sherman of Connecticut before the remaining two members of the Committee echoed the same.

"Is this a graphic figment of your bowlegged imagination?" asked Robert Livingston of New York.

"Or have you suddenly taken up cartography in order to add still another noun to your absurdly long list of credits?" asked Thomas Jefferson of Virginia. "As in 'Benjamin Franklin: founding father, statesman, printer, mapmaker, blah, blah, blah'?" He prattled on in a tone weighted with sarcasm sufficient to drown at least a dozen of his illegitimate children.

With the eight eyes of my fellow Committee members trained on me, I paused to consider precisely how much I should reveal about those maps. As a journalist (lest you have forgotten, I publish the *Pennsylvania Gazette*), I was ethically bound to not disclose my sources. And as a scientist, I was loath to expound on a theory by which I myself was still confounded. Yet, I was more than cognizant they were expectant of a response. Especially John Adams of Massachusetts, who had taken to tugging downward on his left earlobe, as it was quite common knowledge throughout the thirteen colonies that John Adams of Massachusetts possessed a habit of tugging downward on his left earlobe when he was expectant of a response.

I had no ready answer to the question of from where I had procured this map. But at that moment, I chanced to recall an adage that I did not coin but favored anyway. "Necessity Is The Mother of Invention" appears in Plato's *Republic*, and a number of years back I had occasion to pay heed to it when the sun's glare streamed through a pair of bifocals I invented and set some papers upon which they were resting aflame. Finding motivation in that necessity, I invented the Philadelphia Volunteer Fire Department. And while said department did little to neutralize the blaze that rendered my home study a mountainous pile of cinder and ash, its failure did inspire the idea of the lending library, which I then proceeded to invent.

And now it was necessary to devise a credible explanation.

"I will answer that in a moment, gentlemen," I proclaimed. "But not before we all partake in my latest invention, the peanut butter and jelly Claireike!"

"The peanut butter and jelly Claireike?" my esteemed colleagues exclaimed in unison.

"Yes! Let us all celebrate the culmination of our arduous labor as well as the imminence of our Declaration of Independence by partaking in a delicacy that shall be deemed as our new country's first contribution to gastronomy."

"But Benjamin Franklin of Philadelphia," said John Adams of Massachusetts, "did you not bring cutlery, so that we might dine upon your culinary creation like civil beings?"

It was at this juncture that I chortled mightily before announcing, "That is the beauty of this form! For we may sign our Declaration even as we luxuriate in our peanut butter and jelly Claireikes, as this creation is best handled with a single bare hand!"

I then espied a silver letter opener on the writing table, which I grasped and employed to divide the Claireike into five equal pieces. I distributed them among my colleagues, who devoured their portions with a verve heretofore not exhibited in this room. My one regret was the absence of a nearby drum and fife, as I would surely have grabbed and played them to accompany the burgeoning merriment. Instead, however, the Committee made its own music by eating their Claireikes with one hand, while clapping one another's free hands and prancing about the room, singing praises to what will never be known as "the sandwich," thanks to the two of you. And for the first time since the Committee began meeting to draft our Declaration, there was unanimous agreement.

Therefore, as I embark upon my third celebratory potpie, I am overtaken by a feeling of joy and a oneness not only with my future nation but also with my adopted city at the dawn of our new era. The City of Brotherly Love. Philadelphia. A name of literal Greek origin. Compound'd from *phileo*, which means "to love," and *adelphos*, for "brother." I will never forget the doors that opened to me in that very spirit when I arrived here as a wayward young man so many years ago.

So, as I sit by the window here at The Tavern, I swell with anticipation knowing that by seven thirty post meridiem, every literate denizen of these colonies will be perusing the document we completed today. And that Every heart shall be aflame, every soul prepared to fight for his freedom even unto death! By tomorrow's morn, periodicals across the colonies shall take up the message, and soon that old devil King George himself shall see it before him. Our people's truth—history itself—revealed in the making.

Do the two of you have an affinity for potpie? Is it held with the height of regards as a sumptuous delicacy here in the year that you...What is that stirring I see out this Tavern window? It appears to be a gathering, in what has suddenly become a busy street fraught with gatherings and murmurings.

Men, women, and even children are milling about in an Agitated fashion, waving their arms in the air and shouting. Every second, it seems as if more and more people are leaving the wombs of their homes as well as neighboring streets, to spill onto this street. A number of them hold torches.

"What are they so riled about?" I am asking myself. This is not the fervor of revolution. I daresay it is some less wholesome fury that plays upon their faces. And now I see the object that is fomenting such malcontent.

*The Pennsylvania Gazette.*

The special edition of my newspaper that bears the Declaration of Independence on its front page. Which they are reading with scorn in their eyes for reasons that are entirely incomprehensible to me. I am now pressing my expansive forehead against the window and gazing downward to gain a better look at a copy of the *Gazette* that was just strewn about in disgust. And by virtue of the flickering light of a fiery torch being hoisted by a member of this continuously growing mob, I am able to discern an image of the document the Committee of Five composed. All seems fine.

But now a summer gust chances to rise up and blow the paper onto its other side, and what I see arouses consternation sufficient enough for me to lower my fork. It is an image of a map. The very map you submitted in your most recent post to me. The precise map that I displayed to the Committee and that, according to the news copy, arrived at the Gazette affixed to the back of the Declaration by way of a purple-and-tan adhesive, which I suspect to be the trail of peanut butter and grape jelly I personally witnessed taking leave of an excited Roger Sherman of Connecticut's Claireike when he was waving his arms and dancing about, and presumed he was cognizant enough of to dab away.

In Consequence, the printer appears to have thought it part of the document and set it in wax on his printing plate before reproducing thousands of copies, some of them already, no doubt, making their way to other Cities Distant and Near, by way of horse-drawn carriages and the good old Colonial Postal Service, as was the Plan.

And now the agitated cries of the townsfolk are loud in my ears.

"These fellows have hanged us by the neck! We're done for!"

"Naming states that don't even exist? They've lost their minds, the lot of them!"

"King George might not have minded losing thirteen small colonies, but fifty states? For that, he'll crush us!"

"I never trusted that old codger Benjamin Franklin of Philadelphia! Or that comparatively younger codger Thomas Jefferson of Virginia!"

"The shape of this Florida place is obscenely suggestive, I might add."

"This Committee of Five has doomed us! The full might of the Empire will surely be visited upon us, after such a display of ambition!"

"They must answer for themselves!"

Now, my dears Ike and Claire Wanzandae, I fully comprehend their apprehension as I, too, now find myself full of fear for the fate of our colonies if the Mother Country does indeed come to regard our revolt worthy of the full brunt of Her substantial armed forces and weaponry.

This is very, very, very bad.

The people are right. The King shall take notice, and we shall be crushed.

We shall be crushed, and it is my fault.

Yet, there is more.

My torch-flame-illuminated reflection has just been detected through this Tavern window, and the angry mob is pointing in my direction, inching toward me and shouting things like: "Traitor!" "We hate you!" "We hate your high forehead!"

I fear imminent danger to me, Benjamin Franklin, Founding Father, statesman, inventor, printer, author, politician, scientist, musician, philosopher, and creator of the very postal system that delivered the peanut butter and jelly Claireikes that may, indeed, lead to my personal demise.

I am afraid, Ike and Claire Wanzandae, that I have no choice but to continue this letter at a later time, as I must now flee for my life.

I thank the Lord that The Tavern had a back door.

I am not a religious man. I am a scientist for whom faith is eschewed in favor of the empirical. The capacities of my five senses dictate the extent of my beliefs. And the further any stimuli reside from the limits of their perception, the less confidence I have in their veracity.

However, as I witnessed, through the upper half of the bifocals I invented, the mob approaching The Tavern's front door, I dropped to my knees and appealed skyward that the architect who designed that eatery had included a rear exit in his plans.

So now, if my usual penmanship has taken a turn for the illegible, it is because of the turn of events that now finds me writing in the hind seat of a buggy being dragged along the back streets of Philadelphia by what I can only describe as an ancient, swaybacked, famished steed.

HUGE pain in my ▓▓▓▓!

How this has come to pass is remarkably straightforward. I rose from my knees beside my seat by the Tavern's front window, replaced the dessert menu onto the table's top, took one last helping of potpie, and walked hurriedly toward the rear of the restaurant.

As a man of science, I was more than cognizant of the fact that every object in a state of motion tends to remain in that state of motion unless an external force is applied to counteract it. However, as a man of considerable heft, I was also aware that given the increasing speed with which I was traversing the main dining area of The Tavern, I would most assuredly break every Bone in my body upon slamming into the wall of the back room if no door was embedded there. This, of course, would precede the severe pummeling the advancing mob would deliver the instant they caught up and pinned me to that aforementioned wall.

There was a back door. And it was open, no doubt in deference to the extreme humidity of this July night. And because the back room happened to be the Tavern's kitchen, I was fortunate enough, despite the exigencies of this situation, to be able to grab a boysenberry muffin that sat atop a tray that sat atop a counter.

Out the door I went. Once again, all six planets were aligned in my favor: standing at the curb was a horse and buggy, a spacious conveyance that probably belonged to one of The Tavern's patrons who was not being chased at that particular moment.

"Jump in!" exclaimed a rather Young Scamp standing astride the vehicle. Just who this rather Young Scamp might be was of little concern to me at that moment. To my mind, anyone who was not wielding a torch and threatening to insert it into any of my most personal of orifices instantly bore the definition of Ally.

Therefore, without breaking stride, I placed the sole of my left boot onto a stone protruding from the ground, bent slightly about the knees, Vaulted upward and forward, and achieved an altitude I would wager far exceeded any heights heretofore reached by any previous Founding Father, statesman, printer, author, politician, scientist, musician, philosopher, and inventor of the very Franklin stove in which the boysenberry muffin from which I took a healthy bite while airborne had been baked.

At my apogee, I had occasion to glance back at the door, which had just swung open and through which the horde of angry patriots issued, pointing and shouting.

"Traitor!"

"Stringy-haired miscreant!"

"I say, that's my horse and buggy!"

"I say, that's my muffin!"

My descent was precipitous. And devoid of anything I would deem newsworthy when compared to my landing. I came to rest, with a rather resounding plop, in the backseat of the buggy.

"Where would you like to go?" queried the rather Young Scamp.

"I shall defer such a decision to you," I proclaimed. "The operation of such a vehicle does not fall within my vast realm of expertise. What was your desired destination prior to my arrival in this seat in the aft portion of this vehicle?"

"Anywhere so long as it was away from here," he said. "For I am stealing this horse and vehicle and harbor no preference other than to move as quickly as possible."

As the surging crowd was now mere steps away, I beckoned him to take me home and indicated that I would, under these most dire circumstances, be more than pleased to tell him the way.

"Move your chestnut-Colored posterior!" shouted the rather Young Scamp, slapping the leather strap against the quadruped's hind parts.

Whether his admonition was too harsh is not for me to judge. Perhaps it is commonplace for a specimen of that breed to raise his front legs until his entire rearing body is Positioned perpendicular to the ground. And though I made an allowance for the distinct possibility of this phenomenon, as a man of science I am also familiar with Newton's laws of gravity. Thus, I instantly switched to being a man of God and began praying that neither horse nor carriage would tumble backward and reduce myself and my companion to a frothy liquid blend.

My prayers, such as they were, were answered, as the animal instead tipped forward, his front legs reconnecting with the ground, and lurched ahead, leaving behind the reaching arms of those so desirous of ripping me to shreds.

"Make a left upon reaching that quaint Bed-and-Breakfast!" I shouted so as to be heard above the sound of four hoofs clopping rapidly along cobblestone.

In his doing so, I noted with great relief that we had put considerable distance between ourselves and our infuriated pursuers. The comfort and safety of my home was where every Fiber of my being sought refuge, even if it did guarantee the bout with dyspepsia I was certain, thanks to these most extraordinary of circumstances for a Founding Father, statesman, inventor, printer, author, politician, scientist, musician, philosopher, and creator of the postal system, was forthcoming.

All of which delivers me to the present tense, Ike and Claire Wanzandae. Thanks to the speed of the Horse and the skill of the Young Scamp, I can no longer hear the shouts of those colonists who are of a mind to hoist my carcass by a length of rope and beat me with sticks like the very piñata I first encountered in Spain and subsequently popularized in these colonies. I am presently leaning back in my seat and allowing my thoughts to find their inevitable way Home. My home. With a fireplace in every room and a rocking chair (which I invented) lazily placed in front of each of them. Oftentimes, after a long day of printing or inventing or being a statesman, I will take a seat in one of those chairs, lean my head back upon a pillow embroidered with the words *Rest Thy Large Head* and lull myself with thoughts of my childhood in Boston. My first Home. Where, after a long day at school, an interlude of labor at my father's candle shop, and a homemade dinner prepared by my loving Mother, I would retire to the bedroom I shared with my older brother, James, lean back on my pillow and—

What is the noise I am now hearing that has startled me out of my memories of leaning my head against all those pillows? They seem to be sounds emanating from a mob, yet as I look behind me I see no one. This is made more discomforting by the fact that we have just turned the corner onto my own street. I now look forward and espy a throng of irate citizens, brandishing torches and muskets in front of my house and shouting, "Burn it down! Burn it down!"

This new group is far louder than the one that chased us from The Tavern. More irate, and considerably larger, and also with a clearer and more frightful agenda, namely the fiery destruction of my beloved Domicile. My modest abode with my postal box, custom-made in the shape of a kite with an alloyed metal key dangling from its bottom. Said box stands curbside, behind the mob that is now advancing onto my property and trampling the grass as well as the bed of Peonies that I, myself, planted at the foot of the veranda.

"Look!" the rather Young Scamp exclaims while pointing ahead at a raging mass of humanity that is growing before our eyes, their weapons drawn, their deafening chants calling for untold measures of revenge.

"Turn around so they do not see me!" I am begging the rather Young Scamp. "They are not in any mood to reason."

I am frightened, Ike and Claire Wanzandae, and shall now endeavor to increase my efforts at self-concealment by means of a filthy and malodorous blanket lying on this buggy's floor. In view of these exigencies, I promise to finish this missive to you at still *another* time.


"We have arrived!"

After what has seemed like an Eternity under that fetid blanket, I now hear these words of the rather Young Scamp and emerge to see that we are presently at the foot of the steps to Philadelphia's branch of the U.S. Post Office. This was my requested destination. My last spoken words before the Scamp lifted the reins overhead and struck the hide of that compliant horse hard and repeatedly to evade the horde of belligerents who were destroying my beloved home.

"Why are we here?" he would like to know. A logical query, even for a horse-and-buggy thief.

"Because I have a letter I have to mail," I tell him, in regards to the missive I am currently penning to the two of you. "I happen to be a man of my word. Therefore, in spite of the most dire nature of present circumstances, I have every intention of posting this missive to Ike and Claire Wanzandae as promised."

"I know not of Ike and Claire Wanzandae," said the rather Young Scamp. "But I am still in the midst of stealing this horse and buggy and I fear that rowdy crowd will exact their ire on me should they see the two of us together."

As I write these very words, I can hear the approaching din of angry colonists, and feel the vibrations of nearing hoof- and footsteps on the cobblestone beneath this stolen carriage's wheels. So it is with great dispatch that I am now disembarking and racing as fast as these three score plus ten years plus five months plus seventeen days old legs will carry me to the mail depository—so if my penmanship takes still another unfortunate turn for the worse, attribution can be granted to the fact that I am ascending concrete steps at this moment.

"I am off!" shouts the rather Young Scamp, and induces the swaybacked steed to pull away just ahead of the arrival of the surging, riotous mob, who, with torches and firearms in hand, have reached this U.S. Post Office. And who, much to my supreme chagrin, are pointing and shouting hateful epithets in my direction. And now have me encircled, thus blocking all conceivable routes of escape as I place this letter into the mailbox. If the Future has any remedy for this situation, do not hesitate to provide it.

That is to say, Ike and Claire Wanzandae, HELP! HELP HELP HELP.

I am (perhaps not for long),
Benjamin Franklin

# CHAPTER 26

"This is not good," said Claire Wanzandae, who has a gift for understatement.

I didn't say anything, because my throat was filled up with a huge lump that wouldn't move, as if I'd tried to swallow a whole thing of Silly Putty. I thought of poor Benjamin Franklin, standing there in front of the post office, surrounded by a torch-waving mob—a mob so scared that soon a billion British troops were going to arrive on the shores of their country and smash their dreams of freedom to bits that they just wanted to smash something or somebody themselves, get in a few good licks before they took their licking.

Then I thought about that licking. That British smackdown that the good people of Philadelphia and also the not-so-good people of Philadelphia all seemed so sure was coming. What if it happened? Would I still be here? Would the country exist? If it had happened, wouldn't it have happened already? How did any of this work? Was there some point of no return, when the changes we made to the past started to seep forward into the future? Was it like when Carolyn knocked over a full glass of milk and it seeped toward the edge of the table, and if you caught it in time with a sponge, you could keep everything neat, but if it hit that ledge and started dripping down, you were done for?

Maybe the past wasn't a flat surface; maybe it had ledges. Maybe the past was terraced. And maybe King George seeing that newspaper was a ledge. Or Ben Franklin getting murdered or not murdered by a bunch of fire-bearing huckleberries—which was such a horrible thought that I pushed it away for the moment and tried to focus on the bigger picture, the question of whether the past was about to eat up the present and poop a whole different present out the other end. One that might not even have me, or Claire, or Carolyn, or America Itself in it.

Maybe none of that had happened *yet*, because time was like a string connecting the moment BF had mailed that letter to this moment, and as long as it was pulled taut as a tightrope between us, everything between didn't exist.

The lump of Silly Putty wasn't in my throat anymore. It had migrated up to my head and wrapped itself around my brain and started to disintegrate it. These were the kinds of Quandaries that would have made Albert Einstein pee all over himself, and I was no Albert Einstein. I was just a moron with some old-timey stamps and a whole lot of bad ideas.

"This is all our fault," said Claire Wanzandae, who also has a gift for being right about things. I looked into her pretty brown eyes and saw that they were full of tears. "We never should have done it, Ike," she said, and then the first fat drop fell from her eye and splatted on her cheek. I reached out and wiped it away with my thumb, and while I was doing it, another one fell, right onto my hand. It was warm. Almost hot, even. "What if he's dead?" Claire Wanzandae asked, sobbing while she said it so that each syllable stretched out in this awful, choppy, gut-wrenching way.

But somehow, seeing her go to pieces filled me with resolve. The Silly Putty fell away from my brain, and I felt my spine straighten as Determination spread throughout my body.

For once in my life, I knew what I had to do.

"I've got to help him," I told Claire. "He needs me. It's not too late. I know it."

She shook her head back and forth so fast and hard that the tears on her face dried into little streaks of salt water.

"You can't, Ike. It's too dangerous."

I took Claire Wanzandae's hands, and looked into her eyes. Neither of us said anything. We just stared at each other until an Understanding billowed up into the space between us, and I knew that Claire knew that there was nothing she could do to stop me from leaving, and also that she didn't want to stop me anymore. That she knew desperate Times called for desperate Measures and also that the Measure of a man is what he does for his friends, as Benjamin Franklin himself might or might not have said. It is hard to keep Track.

As for me, I could feel a drop of sweat sliding its way slowly down my inner arm. I was terrified of what I was about to do. But I knew I had to Embrace that fear. My country needed me. And more important, so did my friend. If I didn't do something, everything and everyone I loved was in Danger—so much danger that they might not even Exist.

So, like Odysseus in times of yore, I had to leave my peaceful land and lady friend, and go to war. Except, unlike Odysseus, I wasn't going to pretend I was crazy and hitch a donkey and an ox to a plow and sow a field with salt in order to avoid it. Because I am Better than that. And also, I have no plow.

Claire Wanzandae squeezed both my hands and sniffled in a courageous and also adorable manner.

"I believe in you," she said, and those words were probably the best ones I had ever heard.

"Thank you," I said. My heart was soaring around in my chest like a bird that's usually in a cage but suddenly gets let out and flies around the whole house, banging into stuff.

"Let's find you a box," Claire Wanzandae said.

She reached out and brushed something off my face. It was a tear I hadn't even realized I had cried. But that was cool. I wasn't embarrassed at all. Because a Man of Action is allowed to cry, especially when he is about to go Save the world.

# AUTHORS' NOTE

Given that the Esteemed authors of this Volume are best known for writing an obscene fake children's book and a television sketch about a sword-wielding sandwich maker, it might surprise You to learn how much research Went into the writing of this book. The answer is: a little bit. For example, for this one joke about a piñata, Alan e-mailed Adam to point out that maybe piñatas didn't Exist in colonial times, and Adam thought about this for several seconds, Googled "history of piñata," then wrote Alan back to suggest that even if piñatas were not popular in colonial times, Benjamin Franklin traveled frequently to Europe and thus it made sense that he might know about piñatas before Most people, and therefore the joke could be Kept. Alan agreed that this made perfect Sense. The joke eventually got cut for unrelated reasons such as not being that Funny, *but this ought to give you some insight into the level of research the Esteemed authors put into this book, which is not surprising given that they won the Nobel Prize in History in consecutive years.

The Esteemed authors would also like to assure You, the reader, that as Emeritus Professors of Theoretical Physics at Oxford University, they have exceptional insight into the mechanics of time travel, and that all other Matters of both history and science have been Scrutinized and Held to the same standards of accuracy as the part where old stamps cause letters to travel back and forth through time. Which is to say, the Volume you hold in your grubby little hands contains as much fidelity to Factual Reality as was possible without messing up any of the Jokes, or burdening ourselves Unduly. Thank you.

# A NOTE ON THE AUTHORS' NOTE

It has come to the attention of the Esteemed authors that the piñata joke referred to in the Authors' Note actually does appear in this Book after all. We are not sure why we thought it had been cut, although possibly we were Thinking of a different piñata joke, or maybe we took out a pin the tail on the donkey joke or Something. It's all a bit hazy now, to be Honest. In any case, you the Reader have our humble and sincere apologies, and it is our hope that by being Forthright about this delicate and frankly Humiliating matter, we have preserved the sacred Trust necessary for full enjoyment of this otherwise flawlessly rendered and sporadically accurate Tale.

An original *Saturday Night Live* writer, **ALAN ZWEIBEL** has won multiple Emmy and Writers Guild of America awards for his work in television, which also includes *It's Garry Shandling's Show* and *Curb Your Enthusiasm*. On Broadway he collaborated with Billy Crystal on the Tony  Award–winning play *700 Sundays*, and his novel *The Other Shulman* won the 2006 Thurber Prize for American Humor.

**ADAM MANSBACH** is the author of the instant *New York Times* best sellers *Go the \*\*\*\* to Sleep* and *You Have to \*\*\*\*\*\*\* Eat*, as well as the novels *Rage Is Back*, *The Dead Run*, *Angry Black White Boy*, and *The End of the Jews*, winner of the California Book Award. His work has appeared  in *The New Yorker*, *New York Times Book Review*, *Esquire*, *The Believer*, and on National Public Radio's *All Things Considered*.